At the Foot of the Rainbow

By

Gene Stratton-Porter

The Echo Library 2006

Published by

The Echo Library

Echo Library
131 High St.
Teddington
Middlesex TW11 8HH

www.echo-library.com

Please report serious faults in the text to complaints@echo-library.com

ISBN 1-40683-131-X

CONTENTS

GENE STRATTON-PORTER

A LITTLE STORY OF HER LIFE AND WORK

For several years Doubleday, Page & Company have been receiving repeated requests for information about the life and books of Gene Stratton-Porter. Her fascinating nature work with bird, flower, and moth, and the natural wonders of the Limberlost Swamp, made famous as the scene of her nature romances, all have stirred much curiosity among readers everywhere.

Mrs. Porter did not possess what has been called "an aptitude for personal publicity." Indeed, up to the present, she has discouraged quite successfully any attempt to stress the personal note. It is practically impossible, however, to do the kind of work she has done—to make genuine contributions to natural science by her wonderful field work among birds, insects, and flowers, and then, through her romances, to bring several hundred thousands of people to love and understand nature in a way they never did before— without arousing a legitimate interest in her own history, her ideals, her methods of work, and all that underlies the structure of her unusual achievement.

Her publishers have felt the pressure of this growing interest and it was at their request that she furnished the data for a biographical sketch that was to be written of her. But when this actually came to hand, the present compiler found that the author had told a story so much more interesting than anything he could write of her, that it became merely a question of how little need be added.

The following pages are therefore adapted from what might be styled the personal record of Gene Stratton-Porter. This will account for the very intimate picture of family life in the Middle West for some years following the Civil War.

Mark Stratton, the father of Gene Stratton-Porter, described his wife, at the time of their marriage, as a "ninety-pound bit of pink porcelain, pink as a wild rose, plump as a partridge, having a big rope of bright brown hair, never ill a day in her life, and bearing the loveliest name ever given a woman—Mary." He further added that "God fashioned her heart to be gracious, her body to be the mother of children, and as her especial gift of Grace, he put Flower Magic into her fingers." Mary Stratton was the mother of twelve lusty babies, all of whom she reared past eight years of age, losing two a little over that, through an attack of scarlet fever with whooping cough; too ugly a combination for even such a wonderful mother as she. With this brood on her hands she found time to keep an immaculate house, to set a table renowned in her part of the state, to entertain with unfailing hospitality all who came to her door, to beautify her home with such means as she could command, to embroider and fashion clothing by hand for her children; but her great gift was conceded by all to be the making of things to grow. At that she was wonderful. She started dainty little vines and climbing plants from tiny seeds she found in rice and coffee. Rooted things she soaked in water, rolled in fine sand, planted according to habit, and they almost never failed to justify her expectations. She even grew trees and shrubs from slips and cuttings no one else would have thought of trying to cultivate, her last resort being to cut a slip diagonally, insert the lower end in a small potato, and plant as if rooted. And it nearly always grew!

There is a shaft of white stone standing at her head in a cemetery that belonged to her on a corner of her husband's land; but to Mrs. Porter's mind her mother's real monument is a cedar of Lebanon which she set in the manner described above. The cedar tops the brow of a little hill crossing the grounds. She carried two slips from Ohio, where they were given to her by a man who had brought the trees as tiny things from the holy Land. She planted both in this way, one in her dooryard and one in her cemetery. The tree on the hill stands thirty feet tall now, topping all others, and has a trunk two feet in circumference.

Mrs. Porter's mother was of Dutch extraction, and like all Dutch women she worked her special magic with bulbs, which she favoured above other flowers. Tulips, daffodils, star flowers, lilies, dahlias, little bright hyacinths, that she called "blue bells," she dearly loved. From these she distilled exquisite perfume by putting clusters, & time of perfect bloom, in bowls lined with freshly made, unsalted butter, covering them closely, and cutting the few drops of extract thus obtained with alcohol. "She could do more different things," says the author, "and finish them all in a greater degree of perfection than any other woman I have ever known. If I were limited to one adjective in describing her, `capable' would be the word."

The author's father was descended from a long line of ancestors of British blood. he was named for, and traced his origin to, that first Mark Stratton who lived in New York, married the famous beauty, Anne Hutchinson, and settled on Stratton Island, afterward corrupted to Staten, according to family tradition. From that point back for generations across the sea he followed his line to the family of Strattons of which the Earl of Northbrooke is the present head. To his British traditions and the customs of his family, Mark Stratton clung with rigid tenacity, never swerving from his course a particle under the influence of environment or association. All his ideas were clear-cut; no man could influence him against his better judgment. He believed in God, in courtesy, in honour, and cleanliness, in beauty, and in education. He used to say that he would rather see a child of his the author of a book of which he could be proud, than on the throne of England, which was the strongest way he knew to express himself. His very first earnings he spent for a book; when other men rested, he read; all his life he was a student of extraordinarily tenacious memory. He especially loved history: Rollands, Wilson's Outlines, Hume, Macauley, Gibbon, Prescott, and Bancroft, he could quote from all of them paragraphs at a time contrasting the views of different writers on a given event, and remembering dates with unfailing accuracy. "He could repeat the entire Bible," says Mrs. Stratton-Porter, "giving chapters and verses, save the books of Generations; these he said `were a waste of gray matter to learn.' I never knew him to fail in telling where any verse quoted to him was to be found in the Bible." And she adds: "I was almost afraid to make these statements, although there are many living who can corroborate them, until John Muir published the story of his boyhood days, and in it I found the history of such rearing as was my father's, told of as the customary thing among the children of Muir's time; and I have referred many inquirers as to whether this feat were possible, to the Muir book."

All his life, with no thought of fatigue or of inconvenience to himself, Mark Stratton travelled miles uncounted to share what he had learned with those less fortunately situated, by delivering sermons, lectures, talks on civic improvement and politics. To him the love of God could be shown so genuinely in no other way as in the love of his fellowmen. He worshipped beauty: beautiful faces, souls, hearts, beautiful landscapes, trees, animals, flowers. He loved colour: rich, bright colour, and every variation down to the faintest shadings. He was especially fond of red, and the author carefully keeps a cardinal silk handkerchief that he was carrying when stricken with apoplexy at the age of seventy-eight. "It was so like him," she comments, "to have that scrap of vivid colour in his pocket. He never was too busy to fertilize a flower bed or to dig holes for the setting of a tree or bush. A word constantly on his lips was 'tidy.' It applied equally to a woman, a house, a field, or a barn lot. He had a streak of genius in his make-up: the genius of large appreciation. Over inspired Biblical passages, over great books, over sunlit landscapes, over a white violet abloom in deep shade, over a heroic deed of man, I have seen his brow light up, his eyes shine."

Mrs. Porter tells us that her father was constantly reading aloud to his children and to visitors descriptions of the great deeds of men. Two "hair-raisers" she especially remembers with increased heart-beats to this day were the story of John Maynard, who piloted a burning boat to safety while he slowly roasted at the wheel. She says the old thrill comes back when she recalls the inflection of her father's voice as he would cry in imitation of the captain: "John Maynard!" and then give the reply. "Aye, aye, sir!" His other until it sank to a mere gasp: favourite was the story of Clemanthe, and her lover's immortal answer to her question: "Shall we meet again?"

To this mother at forty-six, and this father at fifty, each at intellectual top-notch, every faculty having been stirred for years by the dire stress of Civil War, and the period immediately following, the author was born. From childhood she recalls "thinking things which she felt should be saved," and frequently tugging at her mother's skirts and begging her to "set down" what the child considered stories and poems. Most of these were some big fact in nature that thrilled her, usually expressed in Biblical terms; for the Bible was read twice a day before the family and helpers, and an average of three services were attended on Sunday.

Mrs. Porter says that her first all-alone effort was printed in wabbly letters on the fly-leaf of an old grammar. It was entitled: "Ode to the Moon." "Not," she comments, "that I had an idea what an 'ode' was, other than that I had heard it discussed in the family together with different forms of poetic expression. The spelling must have been by proxy: but I did know the words I used, what they meant, and the idea I was trying to convey.

"No other farm was ever quite so lovely as the one on which I was born after this father and mother had spent twenty-five years beautifying it," says the author. It was called "Hopewell" after the home of some of her father's British ancestors. The natural location was perfect, the land rolling and hilly, with several flowing springs and little streams crossing it in three directions, while plenty of forest still remained. The days of pioneer struggles were past. The roads were smooth and level as floors, the house and barn commodious; the family rode abroad in a double carriage trimmed in patent leather, drawn by a matched team of gray horses, and sometimes the father "speeded a little" for the delight of the children. "We had comfortable clothing," says Mrs. Porter, "and were getting our joy from life without that pinch of anxiety which must have existed in the beginning, although I know that father and mother always held steady, and took a large measure of joy from life in passing."

Her mother's health, which always had been perfect, broke about the time of the author's first remembrance due to typhoid fever contracted after nursing three of her children through it. She lived for several years, but with continual suffering, amounting at times to positive torture.

So it happened, that led by impulse and aided by an escape from the training given her sisters, instead of "sitting on a cushion and sewing a fine seam"—the threads of the fabric had to be counted and just so many allowed to each stitch!—this youngest child of a numerous household spent her waking hours with the wild. She followed her father and the boys afield, and when tired out slept on their coats in fence corners, often awaking with shy creatures peering into her face. She wandered where she pleased, amusing herself with birds, flowers, insects, and plays she invented. "By the day," writes the author, "I trotted from one object which attracted me to another, singing a little song of made-up phrases about everything I saw while I waded catching fish, chasing butterflies over clover fields, or following a bird with a hair in its beak; much of the time I carried the inevitable baby for a woman-child, frequently improvised from an ear of corn in the silk, wrapped in catalpa leaf blankets."

She had a corner of the garden under a big Bartlett pear tree for her very own, and each spring she began by planting radishes and lettuce when the gardening was done; and before these had time to sprout she set the same beds full of spring flowers, and so followed out the season. She made special pets of the birds, locating nest after nest, and immediately projecting herself into the daily life of the occupants. "No one," she says, "ever taught me more than that the birds were useful, a gift of God for our protection from insect pests on fruit and crops; and a gift of Grace in their beauty and music, things to be rigidly protected. From this cue I evolved the idea myself that I must be extremely careful, for had not my father tied a 'kerchief over my mouth when he lifted me for a peep into the nest of the humming-bird, and did he not walk softly and whisper when he approached the spot? So I stepped lightly, made no noise, and watched until I knew what a mother bird fed her young before I began dropping bugs, worms, crumbs, and fruit into little red mouths that opened at my tap on the nest quite as readily as at the touch of the feet of the mother bird."

In the nature of this child of the out-of-doors there ran a fibre of care for wild things. It was instinct with her to go slowly, to touch lightly, to deal lovingly with every living thing: flower, moth, bird, or animal. She never gathered great handfuls of frail wild flowers, carried them an hour and threw them away. If she picked any, she took only a few, mostly to lay on her mother's pillow—for she had a habit of drawing comfort from a cinnamon pink or a trillium laid where its delicate fragrance reached her with every breath. "I am quite sure," Mrs. Porter writes, "that I never in my life, in picking flowers, dragged up the plant by the roots, as I frequently saw other people do. I was taught from infancy to CUT a bloom I wanted. My regular habit was to lift one plant of each kind, especially if it were a species new to me, and set it in my wild-flower garden."

To the birds and flowers the child added moths and butterflies, because she saw them so frequently, the brilliance of colour in yard and garden attracting more than could be found elsewhere. So she grew with the wild, loving, studying, giving all her time. "I fed butterflies sweetened water and rose leaves inside the screen of a cellar window," Mrs. Porter tells us; "doctored all the sick and wounded birds and animals the men brought me from afield; made pets of the baby squirrels and rabbits they carried in for my amusement; collected wild flowers; and as I grew older, gathered arrow points and goose quills for sale in Fort Wayne. So I had the first money I ever earned."

Her father and mother had strong artistic tendencies, although they would have scoffed at the idea themselves, yet the manner in which they laid off their fields, the home they built, the growing things they preserved, the way they planted, the life they led, all go to prove exactly that thing. Their bush—and vine-covered fences crept around the acres they owned in a strip of gaudy colour; their orchard lay in a valley, a square of apple trees in the centre widely bordered by peach, so that it appeared at bloom time like a great pink-bordered white blanket on the face of earth. Swale they might have drained, and would not, made sheets of blue flag, marigold and buttercups. From the home you could not look in any direction without seeing a picture of beauty.

"Last spring," the author writes in a recent letter, "I went back with my mind fully made up to buy that land at any reasonable price, restore it to the exact condition in which I knew it as a child, and finish my life there. I found that the house had been burned, killing all the big trees set by my mother's hands immediately surrounding it. The hills were shorn and ploughed down, filling and obliterating the creeks and springs. Most of the forest had been cut, and stood in corn. My old catalpa in the fence corner beside the road and the Bartlett pear under which I had my wild-flower garden were all that was left of the dooryard, while a few gnarled apple trees remained of the orchard, which had been reset in another place. The garden had been moved, also the lanes; the one creek remaining out of three crossed the meadow at the foot of the orchard. It flowed a sickly current over a dredged bed between bare, straight banks. The whole place seemed worse than a dilapidated graveyard to me. All my love and ten times the money I had at command never could have put back the face of nature as I knew it on that land."

As a child the author had very few books, only three of her own outside of school books. "The markets did not afford the miracles common with the children of today," she adds. "Books are now so numerous, so cheap, and so bewildering in colour and make-up, that I sometimes think our children are losing their perspective and caring for none of them as I loved my few plain little ones filled with short story and poem, almost no illustration. I had a treasure house in the school books of my elders, especially the McGuffey series of Readers from One to Six. For pictures I was driven to the Bible, dictionary, historical works read by my father, agricultural papers, and medical books about cattle and sheep.

"Near the time of my mother's passing we moved from Hopewell to the city of Wabash in order that she might have constant medical attention, and the younger children better opportunities for schooling. Here we had magazines and more books in which I was interested. The one volume in which my heart was enwrapt was a collection of masterpieces of fiction belonging to my eldest sister. It contained 'Paul and Virginia,' 'Undine,' 'Picciola,' 'The Vicar of Wakefield,' 'Pilgrim's Progress,' and several others I soon learned by heart, and the reading and rereading of those exquisitely expressed and conceived stories may have done much in forming high conceptions of what really constitutes literature and in furthering the lofty ideals instilled by my parents. One of these stories formed the basis of my first publicly recognized literary effort."

Reared by people who constantly pointed out every natural beauty, using it wherever possible to drive home a precept, the child lived out-of-doors with the wild almost entirely. If she reported promptly three times a day when the bell rang at meal time, with enough clothing to constitute a decent covering, nothing more was asked until the Sabbath. To be taken from such freedom, her feet shod, her body restricted by as much clothing as ever had been worn on Sunday, shut up in a schoolroom, and set to droning over books, most of which she detested, was the worst punishment ever inflicted upon her she declares. She hated mathematics in any form and spent all her time on natural science, language, and literature. "Friday afternoon," writes Mrs. Porter, "was always taken up with an exercise called 'rhetoricals,' a misnomer as a rule, but let that pass. Each week pupils of one of the four years furnished entertainment for the assembled high school and faculty. Our subjects were always assigned, and we cordially disliked them. This particular day I was to have a paper on 'Mathematical Law.'

"I put off the work until my paper had been called for several times, and so came to Thursday night with excuses and not a line. I was told to bring my work the next morning without fail. I went home in hot anger. Why in all this beautiful world, would they not allow me to do something I could do, and let any one of four members of my class who revelled in mathematics do my subject? That evening I was distracted. 'I can't do a paper on mathematics, and I won't!' I said stoutly; 'but I'll do such a paper on a subject I can write about as will open their foolish eyes and make them see how wrong they are.'"

Before me on the table lay the book I loved, the most wonderful story in which was 'Picciola' by Saintine. Instantly I began to write. Breathlessly I wrote for hours. I exceeded our limit ten times over. The poor Italian Count, the victim of political offences, shut by Napoleon from the wonderful grounds, mansion, and life that were his, restricted to the bare prison walls of Fenestrella, deprived of books and writing material, his one interest in life became a sprout of green, sprung, no doubt, from a seed dropped by a passing bird, between the stone flagging of the prison yard before his window. With him I had watched over it through all the years since I first had access to the book; with him I had prayed for it. I had broken into a cold sweat of fear when the jailer first menaced it; I had hated the wind that bent it roughly, and implored the sun. I had sung a paean of joy at its budding, and worshipped in awe before its thirty perfect blossoms. The Count had named it `Picciola'—the little one—to me also it was a personal possession. That night we lived the life of our `little one' over again, the Count and I, and never were our anxieties and our joys more poignant.

"Next morning," says Mrs. Porter, "I dared my crowd to see how long they could remain on the grounds, and yet reach the assembly room before the last toll of the bell. This scheme worked. Coming in so late the principal opened exercises without remembering my paper. Again, at noon, I was as late as I dared be, and I escaped until near the close of the exercises, through which I sat in cold fear. When my name was reached at last the principal looked at me inquiringly and then announced my inspiring mathematical subject. I arose, walked to the front, and made my best bow. Then I said: `I waited until yesterday because I knew absolutely nothing about my subject'—the audience laughed—`and I could find nothing either here or in the library at home, so last night I reviewed Saintine's masterpiece, "Picciola."'

"Then instantly I began to read. I was almost paralyzed at my audacity, and with each word I expected to hear a terse little interruption. Imagine my amazement when I heard at the end of the first page: `Wait a minute!' Of course I waited, and the principal left the room. A moment later she reappeared accompanied by the superintendent of the city schools. `Begin again,' she said. `Take your time.'

"I was too amazed to speak. Then thought came in a rush. My paper was good. It was as good as I had believed it. It was better than I had known. I did go on! We took that assembly room and the corps of teachers into our confidence, the Count and I, and told them all that was in our hearts about a little flower that sprang between the paving stones of a prison yard. The Count and I were free spirits. From the book I had learned that. He got into political trouble through it, and I had got into mathematical trouble, and we told our troubles. One instant the room was in laughter, the next the boys bowed their heads, and the girls who had forgotten their handkerchiefs cried in their aprons. For almost sixteen big foolscap pages I held them, and I was eager to go on and tell them more about it when I reached the last line. Never again was a subject forced upon me."

After this incident of her schooldays, what had been inclination before was aroused to determination and the child neglected her lessons to write. A volume of crude verse fashioned after the metre of Meredith's "Lucile," a romantic book in rhyme, and two novels were the fruits of this youthful ardour. Through the sickness and death of a sister, the author missed the last three months of school, but, she remarks, "unlike my schoolmates, I studied harder after leaving school than ever before and in a manner that did me real good. The most that can be said of what education I have is that it is the very best kind in the world for me; the only possible kind that would not ruin a person of my inclinations. The others of my family had been to college; I always have been too thankful for words that circumstances intervened which saved my brain from being run through a groove in company with dozens of others of widely different tastes and mentality. What small measure of success I have had has come through preserving my individual point of view, method of expression, and following in after life the Spartan regulations of my girlhood home. Whatever I have been able to do, has been done through the line of education my father saw fit to give me, and through his and my mother's methods of rearing me.

"My mother went out too soon to know, and my father never saw one of the books; but he knew I was boiling and bubbling like a yeast jar in July over some literary work, and if I timidly slipped to him with a composition, or a faulty poem, he saw good in it, and made suggestions for its betterment. When I wanted to express something in colour, he went to an artist, sketched a design for an easel, personally superintended the carpenter who built it, and provided tuition. On that same easel I painted the water colours for 'Moths of the Limberlost,' and one of the most poignant regrets of my life is that he was not there to see them, and to know that the easel which he built through his faith in me was finally used in illustrating a book.

"If I thought it was music through which I could express myself, he paid for lessons and detected hidden ability that should be developed. Through the days of struggle he stood fast; firm in his belief in me. He was half the battle. It was he who demanded a physical standard that developed strength to endure the rigours of scientific field and darkroom work, and the building of ten books in ten years, five of which were on nature subjects, having my own illustrations, and five novels, literally teeming with natural history, true to nature. It was he who demanded of me from birth the finishing of any task I attempted and who taught me to cultivate patience to watch and wait, even years, if necessary, to find and secure material I wanted. It was he who daily lived before me the life of exactly such a man as I portrayed in 'The Harvester,' and who constantly used every atom of brain and body power to help and to encourage all men to do the same."

Marriage, a home of her own, and a daughter for a time filled the author's hands, but never her whole heart and brain. The book fever lay dormant a while, and then it became a compelling influence. It dominated the life she lived, the cabin she designed for their home, and the books she read. When her daughter was old enough to go to school, Mrs. Porter's time came. Speaking of this period, she says: "I could not afford a maid, but I was very strong, vital to the marrow, and I knew how to manage life to make it meet my needs, thanks to even the small amount I had seen of my mother. I kept a cabin of fourteen rooms, and kept it immaculate. I made most of my daughter's clothes, I kept a conservatory in which there bloomed from three to six hundred bulbs every winter, tended a house of canaries and linnets, and cooked and washed dishes besides three times a day. In my spare time (mark the word, there was time to spare else the books never would have been written and the pictures made) I mastered photography to such a degree that the manufacturers of one of our finest brands of print paper once sent the manager of their factory to me to learn how I handled it. He frankly said that they could obtain no such results with it as I did. He wanted to see my darkroom, examine my paraphernalia, and have me tell him exactly how I worked. As I was using the family bathroom for a darkroom and washing negatives and prints on turkey platters in the kitchen, I was rather put to it when it came to giving an exhibition. It was scarcely my fault if men could not handle the paper they manufactured so that it produced the results that I obtained, so I said I thought the difference might lie in the chemical properties of the water, and sent this man on his way satisfied. Possibly it did. But I have a shrewd suspicion it lay in high-grade plates, a careful exposure, judicious development, with self-compounded chemicals straight from the factory, and C.P. I think plates swabbed with wet cotton before development, intensified if of short exposure, and thoroughly swabbed again before drying, had much to do with it; and paper handled in the same painstaking manner had more. I have hundreds of negatives in my closet made twelve years ago, in perfect condition for printing from to-day, and I never have lost a plate through fog from imperfect development and hasty washing; so my little mother's rule of 'whatsoever thy hands find to do, do it with thy might,' held good in photography."

Thus had Mrs. Porter made time to study and to write, and editors began to accept what she sent them with little if any changes. She began by sending photographic and natural history hints to Recreation, and with the first installment was asked to take charge of the department and furnish material each month for which she was to be paid at current prices in high-grade photographic material. We can form some idea of the work she did under this arrangement from the fact that she had over one thousand dollars' worth of equipment at the end of the first year. The second year she increased this by five hundred, and then accepted a place on the natural history staff of Outing, working closely with Mr. Casper Whitney. After a year of this helpful experience Mrs. Porter began to turn her attention to what she calls "nature studies sugar coated with fiction." Mixing some childhood fact with a large degree of grown-up fiction, she wrote a little story entitled "Laddie, the Princess, and the Pie."

"I was abnormally sensitive," says the author, "about trying to accomplish any given thing and failing. I had been taught in my home that it was black disgrace to undertake anything and fail. My husband owned a drug and book store that carried magazines, and it was not possible to conduct departments in any of them and not have it known; but only a few people in our locality read these publications, none of them were interested in nature photography, or natural science, so what I was trying to do was not realized even by my own family.

"With them I was much more timid than with the neighbours. Least of all did I want to fail before my man Person and my daughter and our respective families; so I worked in secret, sent in my material, and kept as quiet about it as possible. On Outing I had graduated from the camera department to an illustrated article each month, and as this kept up the year round, and few illustrations could be made in winter, it meant that I must secure enough photographs of wild life in summer to last during the part of the year when few were to be had.

"Every fair day I spent afield, and my little black horse and load of cameras, ropes, and ladders became a familiar sight to the country folk of the Limberlost, in Rainbow Bottom, the Canoper, on the banks of the Wabash, in woods and thickets and beside the roads; but few people understood what I was trying to do, none of them what it would mean were I to succeed. Being so afraid of failure and the inevitable ridicule in a community where I was already severely criticised on account of my ideas of housekeeping, dress, and social customs, I purposely kept everything I did as quiet as possible. It had to be known that I was interested in everything afield, and making pictures; also that I was writing field sketches for nature publications, but little was thought of it, save as one more, peculiarity, in me. So when my little story was finished I went to our store and looked over the magazines. I chose one to which we did not subscribe, having an attractive cover, good type, and paper, and on the back of an old envelope, behind the counter, I scribbled: Perriton Maxwell, 116 Nassau Street, New York, and sent my story on its way.

"Then I took a bold step, the first in my self-emancipation. Money was beginning to come in, and I had some in my purse of my very own that I had earned when no one even knew I was working. I argued that if I kept my family so comfortable that they missed nothing from their usual routine, it was my right to do what I could toward furthering my personal ambitions in what time I could save from my housework. And until I could earn enough to hire capable people to take my place, I held rigidly to that rule. I who waded morass, fought quicksands, crept, worked from ladders high in air, and crossed water on improvised rafts without a tremor, slipped with many misgivings into the postoffice and rented a box for myself, so that if I met with failure my husband and the men in the bank need not know what I had attempted. That was early May; all summer I waited. I had heard that it required a long time for an editor to read and to pass on matter sent him; but my waiting did seem out of all reason. I was too busy keeping my cabin and doing field work to repine; but I decided in my own mind that Mr. Maxwell was a 'mean old thing' to throw away my story and keep the return postage. Besides, I was deeply chagrined, for I had thought quite well of my effort myself, and this seemed to prove that I did not know even the first principles of what would be considered an interesting story.

"Then one day in September I went into our store on an errand and the manager said to me: 'I read your story in the Metropolitan last night. It was great! Did you ever write any fiction before?'

"My head whirled, but I had learned to keep my own counsels, so I said as lightly as I could, while my heart beat until I feared he could hear it: 'No. Just a simple little thing! Have you any spare copies? My sister might want one.'

"He supplied me, so I hurried home, and shutting myself in the library, I sat down to look my first attempt at fiction in the face. I quite agreed with the manager that it was `great.' Then I wrote Mr. Maxwell a note telling him that I had seen my story in his magazine, and saying that I was glad he liked it enough to use it. I had not known a letter could reach New York and bring a reply so quickly as his answer came. It was a letter that warmed the deep of my heart. Mr. Maxwell wrote that he liked my story very much, but the office boy had lost or destroyed my address with the wrappings, so after waiting a reasonable length of time to hear from me, he had illustrated it the best he could, and printed it. He wrote that so many people had spoken to him of a new, fresh note in it, that he wished me to consider doing him another in a similar vein for a Christmas leader and he enclosed my very first check for fiction.

"So I wrote: `How Laddie and the Princess Spelled Down at the Christmas Bee.' Mr. Maxwell was pleased to accept that also, with what I considered high praise, and to ask me to furnish the illustrations. He specified that he wanted a frontispiece, head and tail pieces, and six or seven other illustrations. Counting out the time for his letter to reach me, and the material to return, I was left with just ONE day in which to secure the pictures. They had to be of people costumed in the time of the early seventies and I was short of print paper and chemicals. First, I telephoned to Fort Wayne for the material I wanted to be sent without fail on the afternoon train. Then I drove to the homes of the people I wished to use for subjects and made appointments for sittings, and ransacked the cabin for costumes. The letter came on the eight A.M. train. At ten o'clock I was photographing Colonel Lupton beside my dining-room fireplace for the father in the story. At eleven I was dressing and posing Miss Lizzie Huart for the princess. At twelve I was picturing in one of my bed rooms a child who served finely for Little Sister, and an hour later the same child in a cemetery three miles in the country where I used mounted butterflies from my cases, and potted plants carried from my conservatory, for a graveyard scene. The time was early November, but God granted sunshine that day, and short focus blurred the background. At four o'clock I was at the schoolhouse, and in the best-lighted room with five or six models, I was working on the spelling bee scenes. By six I was in the darkroom developing and drying these plates, every one of which was good enough to use. I did my best work with printing-out paper, but I was compelled to use a developing paper in this extremity, because it could be worked with much more speed, dried a little between blotters, and mounted. At three o'clock in the morning I was typing the quotations for the pictures, at four the parcel stood in the hall for the six o'clock train, and I realized that I wanted a drink, food, and sleep, for I had not stopped a second for anything from the time of reading Mr. Maxwell's letter until his order was ready to mail. For the following ten years I was equally prompt in doing all work I undertook, whether pictures or manuscript, without a thought of consideration for self; and I disappointed the confident expectations of my nearest and dearest by remaining sane, normal, and almost without exception the healthiest woman they knew."

This story and its pictures were much praised, and in the following year the author was asked for several stories, and even used bird pictures and natural history sketches, quite an innovation for a magazine at that time. With this encouragement she wrote and illustrated a short story of about ten thousand words, and sent it to the Century. Richard Watson Gilder advised Mrs. Porter to enlarge it to book size, which she did. This book is "The Cardinal." Following Mr. Gilder's advice, she recast the tale and, starting with the mangled body of a cardinal some marksman had left in the road she was travelling, in a fervour of love for the birds and indignation at the hunter, she told the Cardinal's life history in these pages.

The story was promptly accepted and the book was published with very beautiful half-tones, and cardinal buckram cover. Incidentally, neither the author's husband nor daughter had the slightest idea she was attempting to write a book until work had progressed to that stage where she could not make a legal contract without her husband's signature. During the ten years of its life this book has gone through eight different editions, varying in form and make-up from the birds in exquisite colour, as colour work advanced and became feasible, to a binding of beautiful red morocco, a number of editions of differing design intervening. One was tried in gray binding, the colour of the female cardinal, with the red male used as an inset. Another was woodsgreen with the red male, and another red with a wild rose design stamped in. There is a British edition published by Hodder and Stoughton. All of these had the author's own illustrations which authorities agree are the most complete studies of the home life and relations of a pair of birds ever published.

The story of these illustrations in "The Cardinal" and how the author got them will be a revelation to most readers. Mrs. Porter set out to make this the most complete set of bird illustrations ever secured, in an effort to awaken people to the wonder and beauty and value of the birds. She had worked around half a dozen nests for two years and had carried a lemon tree from her conservatory to the location of one nest, buried the tub, and introduced the branches among those the birds used in approaching their home that she might secure proper illustrations for the opening chapter, which was placed in the South. When the complete bird series was finished, the difficult work over, and there remained only a few characteristic Wabash River studies of flowers, vines, and bushes for chapter tail pieces to be secured, the author "met her Jonah," and her escape was little short of a miracle.

After a particularly strenuous spring afield, one teeming day in early August she spent the morning in the river bottom beside the Wabash. A heavy rain followed by August sun soon had her dripping while she made several studies of wild morning glories, but she was particularly careful to wrap up and drive slowly going home, so that she would not chill. In the afternoon the author went to the river northeast of town to secure mallow pictures for another chapter, and after working in burning sun on the river bank until exhausted, she several times waded the river to examine bushes on the opposite bank. On the way home she had a severe chill, and for the following three weeks lay twisted in the convulsions of congestion, insensible most of the time. Skilled doctors and nurses did their best, which they admitted would have availed nothing if the patient had not had a constitution without a flaw upon which to work.

"This is the history," said Mrs. Porter, "of one little tail piece among the pictures. There were about thirty others, none so strenuous, but none easy, each having a living, fighting history for me. If I were to give in detail the story of the two years' work required to secure the set of bird studies illustrating 'The Cardinal,' it would make a much larger book than the life of the bird."

"The Cardinal" was published in June of 1903. On the 20th of October, 1904, "Freckles" appeared. Mrs. Porter had been delving afield with all her heart and strength for several years, and in the course of her work had spent every other day for three months in the Limberlost swamp, making a series of studies of the nest of a black vulture. Early in her married life she had met a Scotch lumberman, who told her of the swamp and of securing fine timber there for Canadian shipbuilders, and later when she had moved to within less than a mile of its northern boundary, she met a man who was buying curly maple, black walnut, golden oak, wild cherry, and other wood extremely valuable for a big furniture factory in Grand Rapids. There was one particular woman, of all those the author worked among, who exercised herself most concerning her. She never failed to come out if she saw her driving down the lane to the woods, and caution her to be careful. If she felt that Mrs. Porter had become interested and forgotten that it was long past meal time, she would send out food and water or buttermilk to refresh her. She had her family posted, and if any of them saw a bird with a straw or a hair in its beak, they followed until they found its location. It was her husband who drove the stake and ploughed around the killdeer nest in the cornfield to save it for the author; and he did many other acts of kindness without understanding exactly what he was doing or why. "Merely that I wanted certain things was enough for those people," writes Mrs. Porter. "Without question they helped me in every way their big hearts could suggest to them, because they loved to be kind, and to be generous was natural with them. The woman was busy keeping house and mothering a big brood, and every living creature that came her way, besides. She took me in, and I put her soul, body, red head, and all, into Sarah Duncan. The lumber and furniture man I combined in McLean. Freckles was a composite of certain ideals and my own field experiences, merged with those of Mr. Bob Burdette Black, who, at the expense of much time and careful work, had done more for me than any other ten men afield. The Angel was an idealized picture of my daughter.

"I dedicated the book to my husband, Mr. Charles Darwin Porter, for several reasons, the chiefest being that he deserved it. When word was brought me by lumbermen of the nest of the Black Vulture in the Limberlost, I hastened to tell my husband the wonderful story of the big black bird, the downy white baby, the pale blue egg, and to beg back a rashly made promise not to work in the Limberlost. Being a natural history enthusiast himself, he agreed that I must go; but he qualified the assent with the proviso that no one less careful of me than he, might accompany me there. His business had forced him to allow me to work alone, with hired guides or the help of oilmen and farmers elsewhere; but a Limberlost trip at that time was not to be joked about. It had not been shorn, branded, and tamed. There were most excellent reasons why I should not go there. Much of it was impenetrable. Only a few trees had been taken out; oilmen were just invading it. In its physical aspect it was a treacherous swamp and quagmire filled with every plant, animal, and human danger known in the worst of such locations in the Central States.

"A rod inside the swamp on a road leading to an oil well we mired to the carriage hubs. I shielded my camera in my arms and before we reached the well I thought the conveyance would be torn to pieces and the horse stalled. At the well we started on foot, Mr. Porter in kneeboots, I in waist-high waders. The time was late June; we forced our way between steaming, fetid pools, through swarms of gnats, flies, mosquitoes, poisonous insects, keeping a sharp watch for rattlesnakes. We sank ankle deep at every step, and logs we thought solid broke under us. Our progress was a steady succession of prying and pulling each other to the surface. Our clothing was wringing wet, and the exposed parts of our bodies lumpy with bites and stings. My husband found the tree, cleared the opening to the great prostrate log, traversed its unspeakable odours for nearly forty feet to its farthest recess, and brought the baby and egg to the light in his leaf-lined hat.

"We could endure the location only by dipping napkins in deodorant and binding them over our mouths and nostrils. Every third day for almost three months we made this trip, until Little Chicken was able to take wing. Of course we soon made a road to the tree, grew accustomed to the disagreeable features of the swamp and contemptuously familiar with its dangers, so that I worked anywhere in it I chose with other assistance; but no trip was so hard and disagreeable as the first. Mr. Porter insisted upon finishing the Little Chicken series, so that `deserve' is a poor word for any honour that might accrue to him for his part in the book."

This was the nucleus of the book, but the story itself originated from the fact that one day, while leaving the swamp, a big feather with a shaft over twenty inches long came spinning and swirling earthward and fell in the author's path. Instantly she looked upward to locate the bird, which from the size and formation of the quill could have been nothing but an eagle; her eyes, well trained and fairly keen though they were, could not see the bird, which must have been soaring above range. Familiar with the life of the vulture family, the author changed the bird from which the feather fell to that described in "Freckles." Mrs. Porter had the old swamp at that time practically untouched, and all its traditions to work upon and stores of natural history material. This falling feather began the book which in a few days she had definitely planned and in six months completely written. Her title for it was "The Falling Feather," that tangible thing which came drifting down from Nowhere, just as the boy came, and she has always regretted the change to "Freckles." John Murray publishes a British edition of this book which is even better liked in Ireland and Scotland than in England.

As "The Cardinal" was published originally not by Doubleday, Page & Company, but by another firm, the author had talked over with the latter house the scheme of "Freckles" and it had been agreed to publish the story as soon as Mrs. Porter was ready. How the book finally came to Doubleday, Page & Company she recounts as follows:

"By the time 'Freckles' was finished, I had exercised my woman's prerogative and 'changed my mind'; so I sent the manuscript to Doubleday, Page & Company, who accepted it. They liked it well enough to take a special interest in it and to bring it out with greater expense than it was at all customary to put upon a novel at that time; and this in face of the fact that they had repeatedly warned me that the nature work in it would kill fully half its chances with the public. Mr. F.N. Doubleday, starting on a trip to the Bahamas, remarked that he would like to take a manuscript with him to read, and the office force decided to put 'Freckles' into his grip. The story of the plucky young chap won his way to the heart of the publishers, under a silk cotton tree, 'neath bright southern skies, and made such a friend of him that through the years of its book-life it has been the object of special attention. Mr. George Doran gave me a photograph which Mr. Horace MacFarland made of Mr. Doubleday during this reading of the Mss. of 'Freckles' which is especially interesting."

That more than 2,000,000 readers have found pleasure and profit in Mrs. Porter's books is a cause for particular gratification. These stories all have, as a fundamental reason of their existence, the author's great love of nature. To have imparted this love to others—to have inspired many hundreds of thousands to look for the first time with seeing eyes at the pageant of the out-of-doors—is a satisfaction that must endure. For the part of the publishers, they began their business by issuing "Nature Books" at a time when the sale of such works was problematical. As their tastes and inclinations were along the same lines which Mrs. Porter loved to follow, it gave them great pleasure to be associated with her books which opened the eyes of so great a public to new and worthy fields of enjoyment.

The history of "Freckles" is unique. The publishers had inserted marginal drawings on many pages, but these, instead of attracting attention to the nature charm of the book, seemed to have exactly a contrary effect. The public wanted a novel. The illustrations made it appear to be a nature book, and it required three long slow years for "Freckles" to pass from hand to hand and prove that there really was a novel between the covers, but that it was a story that took its own time and wound slowly toward its end, stopping its leisurely course for bird, flower, lichen face, blue sky, perfumed wind, and the closest intimacies of the daily life of common folk. Ten years have wrought a great change in the sentiment against nature work and the interest in it. Thousands who then looked upon the world with unobserving eyes are now straining every nerve to accumulate enough to be able to end life where they may have bird, flower, and tree for daily companions.

Mrs. Porter's account of the advice she received at this time is particularly interesting. Three editors who read "Freckles" before it was published offered to produce it, but all of them expressed precisely the same opinion: "The book will never sell well as it is. If you want to live from the proceeds of your work, if you want to sell even moderately, you must CUT OUT THE NATURE STUFF." "Now to PUT IN THE NATURE STUFF," continues the author, "was the express purpose for which the book had been written. I had had one year's experience with `The Song of the Cardinal,' frankly a nature book, and from the start I realized that I never could reach the audience I wanted with a book on nature alone. To spend time writing a book based wholly upon human passion and its outworking I would not. So I compromised on a book into which I put all the nature work that came naturally within its scope, and seasoned it with little bits of imagination and straight copy from the lives of men and women I had known intimately, folk who lived in a simple, common way with which I was familiar. So I said to my publishers: `I will write the books exactly as they take shape in my mind. You publish them. I know they will sell enough that you will not lose. If I do not make over six hundred dollars on a book I shall never utter a complaint. Make up my work as I think it should be and leave it to the people as to what kind of book they will take into their hearts and homes.' I altered `Freckles' slightly, but from that time on we worked on this agreement.

"My years of nature work have not been without considerable insight into human nature, as well," continues Mrs. Porter. "I know its failings, its inborn tendencies, its weaknesses, its failures, its depth of crime; and the people who feel called upon to spend their time analyzing, digging into, and uncovering these sources of depravity have that privilege, more's the pity! If I had my way about it, this is a privilege no one could have in books intended for indiscriminate circulation. I stand squarely for book censorship, and I firmly believe that with a few more years of such books, as half a dozen I could mention, public opinion will demand this very thing. My life has been fortunate in one glad way: I have lived mostly in the country and worked in the woods. For every bad man and woman I have ever known, I have met, lived with, and am intimately acquainted with an overwhelming number of thoroughly clean and decent people who still believe in God and cherish high ideals, and it is UPON THE LIVES OF THESE THAT I BASE WHAT I WRITE. To contend that this does not produce a picture true to life is idiocy. It does. It produces a picture true to ideal life; to the best that good men and good women can do at level best.

"I care very little for the magazine or newspaper critics who proclaim that there is no such thing as a moral man, and that my pictures of life are sentimental and idealized. They are! And I glory in them! They are straight, living pictures from the lives of men and women of morals, honour, and loving kindness. They form `idealized pictures of life' because they are copies from life where it touches religion, chastity, love, home, and hope of heaven ultimately. None of these roads leads to publicity and the divorce court. They all end in the shelter and seclusion of a home.

"Such a big majority of book critics and authors have begun to teach, whether they really believe it or not, that no book is TRUE TO LIFE unless it is true to the WORST IN LIFE, that the idea has infected even the women."

In 1906, having seen a few of Mrs. Porter's studies of bird life, Mr. Edward Bok telegraphed the author asking to meet him in Chicago. She had a big portfolio of fine prints from plates for which she had gone to the last extremity of painstaking care, and the result was an order from Mr. Bok for a six months' series in the Ladies' Home Journal of the author's best bird studies accompanied by descriptions of how she secured them. This material was later put in book form under the title, "What I Have Done with Birds," and is regarded as authoritative on the subject of bird photography and bird life, for in truth it covers every phase of the life of the birds described, and contains much of other nature subjects.

By this time Mrs. Porter had made a contract with her publishers to alternate her books. She agreed to do a nature book for love, and then, by way of compromise, a piece of nature work spiced with enough fiction to tempt her class of readers. In this way she hoped that they would absorb enough of the nature work while reading the fiction to send them afield, and at the same time keep in their minds her picture of what she considers the only life worth living. She was still assured that only a straight novel would "pay," but she was living, meeting all her expenses, giving her family many luxuries, and saving a little sum for a rainy day she foresaw on her horoscope. To be comfortably clothed and fed, to have time and tools for her work, is all she ever has asked of life.

Among Mrs. Porter's readers "At the Foot of the Rainbow" stands as perhaps the author's strongest piece of fiction.

In August of 1909 two books on which the author had been working for years culminated at the same time: a nature novel, and a straight nature book. The novel was, in a way, a continuation of "Freckles," filled as usual with wood lore, but more concerned with moths than birds. Mrs. Porter had been finding and picturing exquisite big night flyers during several years of field work among the birds, and from what she could have readily done with them she saw how it would be possible for a girl rightly constituted and environed to make a living, and a good one, at such work. So was conceived "A Girl of the Limberlost." "This comes fairly close to my idea of a good book," she writes. "No possible harm can be done any one in reading it. The book can, and does, present a hundred pictures that will draw any reader in closer touch with nature and the Almighty, my primal object in each line I write. The human side of the book is as close a character study as I am capable of making. I regard the character of Mrs. Comstock as the best thought-out and the cleanest-cut study of human nature I have so far been able to do. Perhaps the best justification of my idea of this book came to me recently when I received an application from the President for permission to translate it into Arabic, as the first book to be used in an effort to introduce our methods of nature study into the College of Cairo."

Hodder and Stoughton of London published the British edition of this work.

At the same time that "A Girl of the Limberlost" was published there appeared the book called "Birds of the Bible." This volume took shape slowly. The author made a long search for each bird mentioned in the Bible, how often, where, why; each quotation concerning it in the whole book, every abstract reference, why made, by whom, and what it meant. Then slowly dawned the sane and true things said of birds in the Bible compared with the amazing statements of Aristotle, Aristophanes, Pliny, and other writers of about the same period in pagan nations. This led to a search for the dawn of bird history and for the very first pictures preserved of them. On this book the author expended more work than on any other she has ever written.

In 1911 two more books for which Mrs. Porter had gathered material for long periods came to a conclusion on the same date: "Music of the Wild" and "The Harvester." The latter of these was a nature novel; the other a frank nature book, filled with all outdoors—a special study of the sounds one hears in fields and forests, and photographic reproductions of the musicians and their instruments.

The idea of "The Harvester" was suggested to the author by an editor who wanted a magazine article, with human interest in it, about the ginseng diggers in her part of the country. Mr. Porter had bought ginseng for years for a drug store he owned; there were several people he knew still gathering it for market, and growing it was becoming a good business all over the country. Mrs. Porter learned from the United States Pharmacopaeia and from various other sources that the drug was used mostly by the Chinese, and with a wholly mistaken idea of its properties. The strongest thing any medical work will say for ginseng is that it is "A VERY MILD AND SOOTHING DRUG." It seems that the Chinese buy and use it in enormous quantities, in the belief that it is a remedy for almost every disease to which humanity is heir; that it will prolong life, and that it is a wonderful stimulant. Ancient medical works make this statement, laying special emphasis upon its stimulating qualities. The drug does none of these things. Instead of being a stimulant, it comes closer to a sedative. This investigation set the author on the search for other herbs that now are or might be grown as an occupation. Then came the idea of a man who should grow these drugs professionally, and of the sick girl healed by them. "I could have gone to work and started a drug farm myself," remarks Mrs. Porter, "with exactly the same profit and success as the Harvester. I wrote primarily to state that to my personal knowledge, clean, loving men still exist in this world, and that no man is forced to endure the grind of city life if he wills otherwise. Any one who likes, with even such simple means as herbs he can dig from fence corners, may start a drug farm that in a short time will yield him delightful work and independence. I WROTE THE BOOK AS I THOUGHT IT SHOULD BE WRITTEN, TO PROVE MY POINTS AND ESTABLISH MY CONTENTIONS. I THINK IT DID. MEN THE GLOBE AROUND PROMPTLY WROTE ME THAT THEY ALWAYS HAD OBSERVED THE MORAL CODE; OTHERS THAT THE SUBJECT NEVER IN ALL THEIR LIVES HAD BEEN PRESENTED TO THEM FROM MY POINT OF VIEW, BUT NOW THAT IT HAD BEEN, THEY WOULD CHANGE AND DO WHAT THEY COULD TO INFLUENCE ALL MEN TO DO THE SAME"

Messrs. Hodder and Stoughton publish a British edition of "The Harvester," there is an edition in Scandinavian, it was running serially in a German magazine, but for a time at least the German and French editions that were arranged will be stopped by this war, as there was a French edition of "The Song of the Cardinal."

After a short rest, the author began putting into shape a book for which she had been compiling material since the beginning of field work. From the first study she made of an exquisite big night moth, Mrs. Porter used every opportunity to secure more and representative studies of each family in her territory, and eventually found the work so fascinating that she began hunting cocoons and raising caterpillars in order to secure life histories and make illustrations with fidelity to life. "It seems," comments the author, "that scientists and lepidopterists from the beginning have had no hesitation in describing and using mounted moth and butterfly specimens for book text and illustration, despite the fact that their colours fade rapidly, that the wings are always in unnatural positions, and the bodies shrivelled. I would quite as soon accept the mummy of any particular member of the Rameses family as a fair representation of the living man, as a mounted moth for a live one."

When she failed to secure the moth she wanted in a living and perfect specimen for her studies, the author set out to raise one, making photographic studies from the eggs through the entire life process. There was one June during which she scarcely slept for more than a few hours of daytime the entire month. She turned her bedroom into a hatchery, where were stored the most precious cocoons; and if she lay down at night it was with those she thought would produce moths before morning on her pillow, where she could not fail to hear them emerging. At the first sound she would be up with notebook in hand, and by dawn, busy with cameras. Then she would be forced to hurry to the darkroom and develop her plates in order to be sure that she had a perfect likeness, before releasing the specimen, for she did release all she produced except one pair of each kind, never having sold a moth, personally. Often where the markings were wonderful and complicated, as soon as the wings were fully developed Mrs. Porter copied the living specimen in water colours for her illustrations, frequently making several copies in order to be sure that she laid on the colour enough BRIGHTER than her subject so that when it died it would be exactly the same shade.

"Never in all my life," writes the author, "have I had such exquisite joy in work as I had in painting the illustrations for this volume of 'Moths of the Limberlost.' Colour work had advanced to such a stage that I knew from the beautiful reproductions in Arthur Rackham's 'Rheingold and Valkyrie' and several other books on the market, that time so spent would not be lost. Mr. Doubleday had assured me personally that I might count on exact reproduction, and such details of type and paper as I chose to select. I used the easel made for me when a girl, under the supervision of my father, and I threw my whole heart into the work of copying each line and delicate shading on those wonderful wings, 'all diamonded with panes of quaint device, innumerable stains and splendid dyes,' as one poet describes them. There were times, when in working a mist of colour over another background, I cut a brush down to three hairs. Some of these illustrations I sent back six and seven times, to be worked over before the illustration plates were exact duplicates of the originals, and my heart ached for the engravers, who must have had Job-like patience; but it did not ache enough to stop me until I felt the reproduction exact. This book tells its own story of long and patient waiting for a specimen, of watching, of disappointments, and triumphs. I love it especially among my book children because it represents my highest ideals in the making of a nature book, and I can take any skeptic afield and prove the truth of the natural history it contains."

In August of 1913 the author's novel "Laddie" was published in New York, London, Sydney and Toronto simultaneously. This book contains the same mixture of romance and nature interest as the others, and is modelled on the same plan of introducing nature objects peculiar to the location, and characters, many of whom are from life, typical of the locality at a given period. The first thing many critics said of it was that "no such people ever existed, and no such life was ever lived." In reply to this the author said: "Of a truth, the home I described in this book I knew to the last grain of wood in the doors, and I painted, it with absolute accuracy; and many of the people I described I knew more intimately than I ever have known any others. TAKEN AS A WHOLE IT REPRESENTS A PERFECTLY FAITHFUL PICTURE OF HOME LIFE, IN A FAMILY WHO WERE REARED AND EDUCATED EXACTLY AS THIS BOOK INDICATES. There was such a man as Laddie, and he was as much bigger and better than my description of him as a real thing is always better than its presentment. The only difference, barring the nature work, between my books and those of many other writers, is that I prefer to describe and to perpetuate the BEST I have known in life; whereas many authors seem to feel that they have no hope of achieving a high literary standing unless they delve in and reproduce the WORST.

"To deny that wrong and pitiful things exist in life is folly, but to believe that these things are made better by promiscuous discussion at the hands of writers who FAIL TO PROVE BY THEIR BOOKS that their viewpoint is either right, clean, or helpful, is close to insanity. If there is to be any error on either side in a book, then God knows it is far better that it should be upon the side of pure sentiment and high ideals than upon that of a too loose discussion of subjects which often open to a large part of the world their first knowledge of such forms of sin, profligate expenditure, and waste of life's best opportunities. There is one great beauty in idealized romance: reading it can make no one worse than he is, while it may help thousands to a cleaner life and higher inspiration than they ever before have known."

Mrs. Porter has written ten books, and it is not out of place here to express her attitude toward them. Each was written, she says, from her heart's best impulses. They are as clean and helpful as she knew how to make them, as beautiful and interesting. She has never spared herself in the least degree, mind or body, when it came to giving her best, and she has never considered money in relation to what she was writing.

During the hard work and exposure of those early years, during rainy days and many nights in the darkroom, she went straight ahead with field work, sending around the globe for books and delving to secure material for such books as "Birds of the Bible," "Music of the Wild," and "Moths of the Limberlost." Every day devoted to such work was "commercially" lost, as publishers did not fail to tell her. But that was the work she could do, and do with exceeding joy. She could do it better pictorially, on account of her lifelong knowledge of living things afield, than any other woman had as yet had the strength and nerve to do it. It was work in which she gloried, and she persisted. "Had I been working for money," comments the author, "not one of these nature books ever would have been written, or an illustration made."

When the public had discovered her and given generous approval to "A Girl of the Limberlost," when "The Harvester" had established a new record, that would have been the time for the author to prove her commercialism by dropping nature work, and plunging headlong into books it would pay to write, and for which many publishers were offering alluring sums. Mrs. Porter's answer was the issuing of such books as "Music of the Wild" and "Moths of the Limberlost." No argument is necessary. Mr. Edward Shuman, formerly critic of the Chicago Record-Herald, was impressed by this method of work and pointed it out in a review. It appealed to Mr. Shuman, when "Moths of the Limberlost" came in for review, following the tremendous success of "The Harvester," that had the author been working for money, she could have written half a dozen more "Harvesters" while putting seven years of field work, on a scientific subject, into a personally illustrated work.

In an interesting passage dealing with her books, Mrs. Porter writes: "I have done three times the work on my books of fiction that I see other writers putting into a novel, in order to make all natural history allusions accurate and to write them in such fashion that they will meet with the commendation of high schools, colleges, and universities using what I write as text books, and for the homes that place them in their libraries. I am perfectly willing to let time and the hearts of the people set my work in its ultimate place. I have no delusions concerning it.

"To my way of thinking and working the greatest service a piece of fiction can do any reader is to leave him with a higher ideal of life than he had when he began. If in one small degree it shows him where he can be a gentler, saner, cleaner, kindlier man, it is a wonder-working book. If it opens his eyes to one beauty in nature he never saw for himself, and leads him one step toward the God of the Universe, it is a beneficial book, for one step into the miracles of nature leads to that long walk, the glories of which so strengthen even a boy who thinks he is dying, that he faces his struggle like a gladiator."

During the past ten years thousands of people have sent the author word that through her books they have been led afield and to their first realization of the beauties of nature her mail brings an average of ten such letters a day, mostly from students, teachers, and professional people of our largest cities. It can probably be said in all truth of her nature books and nature novels, that in the past ten years they have sent more people afield than all the scientific writings of the same period. That is a big statement, but it is very likely pretty close to the truth. Mrs. Porter has been asked by two London and one Edinburgh publishers for the privilege of bringing out complete sets of her nature books, but as yet she has not felt ready to do this.

In bringing this sketch of Gene Stratton-Porter to a close it will be interesting to quote the author's own words describing the Limberlost Swamp, its gradual disappearance under the encroachments of business, and her removal to a new field even richer in natural beauties. She says: "In the beginning of the end a great swamp region lay in northeastern Indiana. Its head was in what is now Noble and DeKalb counties; its body in Allen and Wells, and its feet in southern Adams and northern Jay The Limberlost lies at the foot and was, when I settled near it, EXACTLY AS DESCRIBED IN MY BOOKS. The process of dismantling it was told in, Freckles, to start with, carried on in `A Girl of the Limberlost,' and finished in `Moths of the Limberlost.' Now it has so completely fallen prey to commercialism through the devastation of lumbermen, oilmen, and farmers, that I have been forced to move my working territory and build a new cabin about seventy miles north, at the head of the swamp in Noble county, where there are many lakes, miles of unbroken marsh, and a far greater wealth of plant and animal life than existed during my time in the southern part. At the north end every bird that frequents the Central States is to be found. Here grow in profusion many orchids, fringed gentians, cardinal flowers, turtle heads, starry campions, purple gerardias, and grass of Parnassus. In one season I have located here almost every flower named in the botanies as native to these regions and several that I can find in no book in my library.

"But this change of territory involves the purchase of fifteen acres of forest and orchard land, on a lake shore in marsh country. It means the building of a permanent, all-year-round home, which will provide the comforts of life for my family and furnish a workshop consisting of a library, a photographic darkroom and negative closet, and a printing room for me. I could live in such a home as I could provide on the income from my nature work alone; but when my working grounds were cleared, drained and ploughed up, literally wiped from the face of the earth, I never could have moved to new country had it not been for the earnings of the novels, which I now spend, and always have spent, in great part UPON MY NATURE WORK. Based on this plan of work and life I have written ten books, and `please God I live so long,' I shall write ten more. Possibly every one of them will be located in northern Indiana. Each one will be filled with all the field and woods legitimately falling to its location and peopled with the best men and women I have known."

Chapter 1

THE RAT-CATCHERS OF THE WABASH

"HEY, you swate-scented little heart-warmer!" cried Jimmy Malone, as he lifted his tenth trap, weighted with a struggling muskrat, from the Wabash. "Varmint you may be to all the rist of creation, but you mane a night at Casey's to me."

Jimmy whistled softly as he reset the trap. For the moment he forgot that he was five miles from home, that it was a mile farther to the end of his line at the lower curve of Horseshoe Bend, that his feet and fingers were almost freezing, and that every rat of the ten now in the bag on his back had made him thirstier. He shivered as the cold wind sweeping the curves of the river struck him; but when an unusually heavy gust dropped the ice and snow from a branch above him on the back of his head, he laughed, as he ducked and cried: "Kape your snowballing till the Fourth of July, will you!"

"Chick-a-dee-dee-dee!" remarked a tiny gray bird on the tree above him. Jimmy glanced up. "Chickie, Chickie, Chickie," he said. "I can't till by your dress whether you are a hin or a rooster. But I can till by your employmint that you are working for grub. Have to hustle lively for every worm you find, don't you, Chickie? Now me, I'm hustlin' lively for a drink, and I be domn if it seems nicessary with a whole river of drinkin' stuff flowin' right under me feet. But the old Wabash ain't runnin "wine and milk and honey" not by the jug-full. It seems to be compounded of aquil parts of mud, crude ile, and rain water. If 'twas only runnin' Melwood, be gorry, Chickie, you'd see a mermaid named Jimmy Malone sittin' on the Kingfisher Stump, combin' its auburn hair with a breeze, and scoopin' whiskey down its gullet with its tail fin. No, hold on, Chickie, you wouldn't either. I'm too flat-chisted for a mermaid, and I'd have no time to lave off gurglin' for the hair-combin' act, which, Chickie, to me notion is as issential to a mermaid as the curves. I'd be a sucker, the biggest sucker in the Gar-hole, Chickie bird. I'd be an all-day sucker, be gobs; yis, and an all- night sucker, too. Come to think of it, Chickie, be domn if I'd be a sucker at all. Look at the mouths of them! Puckered up with a drawstring! Oh, Hell on the Wabash, Chickie, think of Jimmy Malone lyin' at the bottom of a river flowin' with Melwood, and a puckerin'-string mouth! Wouldn't that break the heart of you? I know what I'd be. I'd be the Black Bass of Horseshoe Bend, Chickie, and I'd locate just below the shoals headin' up stream, and I'd hold me mouth wide open till I paralyzed me jaws so I couldn't shut thim. I'd just let the pure stuff wash over me gills constant, world without end. Good-by, Chickie. Hope you got your grub, and pretty soon I'll have enough drink to make me feel like I was the Bass for one night, anyway."

Jimmy hurried to his next trap, which was empty, but the one after that contained a rat, and there were footprints in the snow. "That's where the porrage-heart of the Scotchman comes in," said Jimmy, as he held up the rat by one foot, and gave it a sharp rap over the head with the trap to make sure it was dead. "Dannie could no more hear a rat fast in one of me traps and not come over and put it out of its misery, than he could dance a hornpipe. And him only sicond hand from hornpipe land, too! But his feet's like lead. Poor Dannie! He gets just about half the rats I do. He niver did have luck."

Jimmy's gay face clouded for an instant. The twinkle faded from his eyes, and a look of unrest swept into them. He muttered something, and catching up his bag, shoved in the rat. As he reset the trap, a big crow dropped from branch to branch on a sycamore above him, and his back scarcely was turned before it alighted on the ice, and ravenously picked at three drops of blood purpling there.

Away down the ice-sheeted river led Dannie's trail, showing plainly across the snow blanket. The wind raved through the trees, and around the curves of the river. The dark earth of the banks peeping from under overhanging ice and snow, looked like the entrance to deep mysterious caves. Jimmy's superstitious soul readily peopled them with goblins and devils. He shuddered, and began to talk aloud to cheer himself. "Elivin muskrat skins, times fifteen cints apiece, one dollar sixty-five. That will buy more than I can hold. Hagginy! Won't I be takin' one long fine gurgle of the pure stuff! And there's the boys! I might do the grand for once. One on me for the house! And I might pay something on my back score, but first I'll drink till I swell like a poisoned pup. And I ought to get Mary that milk pail she's been kickin' for this last month. Women and cows are always kickin'! If the blarsted cow hadn't kicked a hole in the pail, there'd be no need of Mary kicking for a new one. But dough IS dubious soldering. Mary says it's bad enough on the dish pan, but it positively ain't hilthy about the milk pail, and she is right. We ought to have a new pail. I guess I'll get it first, and fill up on what's left. One for a quarter will do. And I've several traps yet, I may get a few more rats."

The virtuous resolve to buy a milk pail before he quenched the thirst which burned him, so elated Jimmy with good opinion of himself that he began whistling gayly as he strode toward his next trap. And by that token, Dannie Macnoun, resetting an empty trap a quarter of a mile below, knew that Jimmy was coming, and that as usual luck was with him. Catching his blood and water dripping bag, Dannie dodged a rotten branch that came crashing down under the weight of its icy load, and stepping out on the river, he pulled on his patched wool-lined mittens as he waited for Jimmy.

"How many, Dannie?" called Jimmy from afar.

"Seven," answered Dannie. "What for ye?"

"Elivin," replied Jimmy, with a bit of unconscious swagger. "I am havin' poor luck to-day."

"How mony wad satisfy ye?" asked Dannie sarcastically.

"Ain't got time to figure that," answered Jimmy, working in a double shuffle as he walked. "Thrash around a little, Dannie. It will warm you up."

"I am no cauld," answered Dannie.

"No cauld!" imitated Jimmy. "No cauld! Come to observe you closer, I do detect symptoms of sunstroke in the ridness of your face, and the whiteness about your mouth; but the frost on your neck scarf, and the icicles fistooned around the tail of your coat, tell a different story.

"Dannie, you remind me of the baptizin' of Pete Cox last winter. Pete's nothin' but skin and bone, and he niver had a square meal in his life to warm him. It took pushin' and pullin' to get him in the water, and a scum froze over while he was under. Pete came up shakin' like the feeder on a thrashin' machine, and whin he could spake at all, `Bless Jasus,' says he, `I'm jist as wa-wa-warm as I wa-wa-want to be.' So are you, Dannie, but there's a difference in how warm folks want to be. For meself, now, I could aisily bear a little more hate."

"It's honest, I'm no cauld," insisted Dannie; and he might have added that if Jimmy would not fill his system with Casey's poisons, that degree of cold would not chill and pinch him either. But being Dannie, he neither thought nor said it. "'Why, I'm frozen to me sowl!" cried Jimmy, as he changed the rat bag to his other hand, and beat the empty one against his leg." Say, Dannie, where do you think the Kingfisher is wintering?"

"And the Black Bass," answered Dannie. "Where do ye suppose the Black Bass is noo?"

"Strange you should mintion the Black Bass," said Jimmy. "I was just havin' a little talk about him with a frind of mine named Chickie-dom, no, Chickie-dee, who works a grub stake back there.

The Bass might be lyin' in the river bed right under our feet. Don't you remimber the time whin I put on three big cut-worms, and skittered thim beyond the log that lays across here, and he lept from the water till we both saw him the best we ever did, and nothin' but my old rotten line ever saved him? Or he might be where it slumps off just below the Kingfisher stump. But I know where he is all right. He's down in the Gar-hole, and he'll come back here spawning time, and chase minnows when the Kingfisher comes home. But, Dannie, where the nation do you suppose the Kingfisher is?"

"No' so far away as ye might think," replied Dannie. "Doc Hues told me that coming on the train frae Indianapolis on the fifteenth of December, he saw one fly across a little pond juist below Winchester. I believe they go south slowly, as the cold drives them, and stop near as they can find guid fishing. Dinna that stump look lonely wi'out him?"

"And sound lonely without the Bass slashing around! I am going to have that Bass this summer if I don't do a thing but fish!" vowed Jimmy.

"I'll surely have a try at him," answered Dannie, with a twinkle in his gray eyes. "We've caught most everything else in the Wabash, and our reputation fra taking guid fish is ahead of any one on the river, except the Kingfisher. Why the Diel dinna one of us haul out that Bass?"

"Ain't I just told you that I am going to hook him this summer?" shivered Jimmy.

"Dinna ye hear me mention that I intended to take a try at him mysel'?" questioned Dannie. "Have ye forgotten that I know how to fish?"

"'Nough breeze to-day without starting a Highlander," interposed Jimmy hastily. "I believe I hear a rat in my next trap. That will make me twilve, and it's good and glad of it I am for I've to walk to town when my line is reset. There's something Mary wants."

"If Mary wants ye to go to town, why dinna ye leave me to finish your traps, and start now?" asked Dannie. "It's getting dark, and if ye are so late ye canna see the drifts, ye never can cut across the fields; fra the snow is piled waist high, and it's a mile farther by the road."

"I got to skin my rats first, or I'll be havin' to ask credit again," replied Jimmy.

"That's easy," answered Dannie. "Turn your rats over to me richt noo. I'll give ye market price fra them in cash."

"But the skinnin' of them," objected Jimmy for decency sake, though his eyes were beginning to shine and his fingers to tremble.

"Never ye mind about that," retorted Dannie. "I like to take my time to it, and fix them up nice. Elivin, did ye say?"

"Elivin," answered Jimmy, breaking into a jig, supposedly to keep his feet warm, in reality because he could not stand quietly while Dannie pulled off his mittens, got out and unstrapped his wallet, and carefully counted out the money. "Is that all ye need?" he asked.

For an instant Jimmy hesitated. Missing a chance to get even a few cents more meant a little shorter time at Casey's. "That's enough, I think," he said. "I wish I'd staid out of matrimony, and then maybe I could iver have a cint of me own. You ought to be glad you haven't a woman to consume ivery penny you earn before it reaches your pockets, Dannie Micnoun."

"I hae never seen Mary consume much but calico and food," Dannie said dryly.

"Oh, it ain't so much what a woman really spinds," said Jimmy, peevishly, as he shoved the money into his pocket, and pulled on his mittens. "It's what you know she would spind if she had the chance."

"I dinna think ye'll break up on that," laughed Dannie.

And that was what Jimmy wanted. So long as he could set Dannie laughing, he could mold him.

"No, but I'll break down," lamented Jimmy in sore self-pity, as he remembered the quarter sacred to the purchase of the milk pail.

"Ye go on, and hurry," urged Dannie. "If ye dinna start home by seven, I'll be combing the drifts fra ye before morning."

"Anything I can do for you?" asked Jimmy, tightening his old red neck scarf.

"Yes," answered Dannie. "Do your errand and start straight home, your teeth are chattering noo. A little more exposure, and the rheumatism will be grinding ye again. Ye will hurry, Jimmy?"

"Sure!" cried Jimmy, ducking under a snow slide, and breaking into a whistle as he turned toward the road.

Dannie's gaze followed Jimmy's retreating figure until he climbed the bank, and was lost in the woods, and the light in his eyes was the light of love. He glanced at the sky, and hurried down the river. First across to Jimmy's side to gather his rats and reset his traps, then to his own. But luck seemed to have turned, for all the rest of Dannie's were full, and all of Jimmy's were empty. But as he was gone, it was not necessary for Dannie to slip across and fill them, as was his custom when they worked together. He would divide the rats at skinning time, so that Jimmy would have just twice as many as he, because Jimmy had a wife to support. The last trap of the line lay a little below the curve of Horseshoe Bend, and there Dannie twisted the tops of the bags together, climbed the bank, and struck across Rainbow Bottom. He settled his load to his shoulders, and glanced ahead to choose the shortest route. He stopped suddenly with a quick intake of breath.

"God!" he cried reverently. "Hoo beautifu' are Thy works."

The ice-covered Wabash circled Rainbow Bottom like a broad white frame, and inside it was a perfect picture wrought in crystal white and snow shadows. The blanket on the earth lay smoothly in even places, rose with knolls, fell with valleys, curved over prostrate logs, heaped in mounds where bushes grew thickly, and piled high in drifts where the wind blew free. In the shelter of the bottom the wind had not stripped the trees of their loads as it had those along the river. The willows, maples, and soft woods bent almost to earth with their shining burden; but the stout, stiffly upstanding trees, the oaks, elms, and cottonwoods defied the elements to bow their proud heads. While the three mighty trunks of the great sycamore in the middle looked white as the snow, and dwarfed its companions as it never had in summer; its wide-spreading branches were sharply cut against the blue background, and they tossed their frosted balls in the face of Heaven. The giant of Rainbow Bottom might be broken, but it never would bend. Every clambering vine, every weed and dried leaf wore a coat of lace-webbed frostwork. The wind swept a mist of tiny crystals through the air, and from the shelter of the deep woods across the river a Cardinal whistled gayly.

The bird of Good Cheer, whistling no doubt on an empty crop, made Dannie think of Jimmy, and his unfailing fountain of mirth. Dear Jimmy! Would he ever take life seriously? How good he was to tramp to town and back after five miles on the ice. He thought of Mary with almost a touch of impatience. What did the woman want that was so necessary as to send a man to town after a day on the ice? Jimmy would be dog tired when he got home. Dannie decided to hurry, and do the feeding and get in the wood before he began to skin the rats.

He found walking uncertain. He plunged into unsuspected hollows, and waded drifts, so that he was panting when he reached the lane. From there he caught the gray curl of smoke against the sky from one of two log cabins side by side at the top of the embankment, and he almost ran toward them. Mary might think they were late at the traps, and be out doing the feeding, and it would be cold for a woman.

On reaching his own door, he dropped the rat bags inside, and then hurried to the yard of the other cabin. He gathered a big load of wood in his arms, and stamping the snow from his feet, called "Open!" at the door. Dannie stepped inside and filled the empty box. With smiling eyes he turned to Mary, as he brushed the snow and moss from his sleeves.

"Nothing but luck to-day," he said. "Jimmy took elivin fine skins frae his traps before he started to town, and I got five more that are his, and I hae eight o' my own."

Mary looked such a dream to Dannie, standing there all pink and warm and tidy in her fresh blue dress, that he blinked and smiled, half bewildered.

"What did Jimmy go to town for?" she asked.

"Whatever it was ye wanted," answered Dannie.

"What was it I wanted?" persisted Mary.

"He dinna tell me," replied Dannie, and the smile wavered.

"Me, either," said Mary, and she stooped and picked up her sewing.

Dannie went out and gently closed the door. He stood for a second on the step, forcing himself to take an inventory of the work. There were the chickens to feed, and the cows to milk, feed, and water. Both the teams must be fed and bedded, a fire in his own house made, and two dozen rats skinned, and the skins put to stretch and cure. And at the end of it all, instead of a bed and rest, there was every probability that he must drive to town after Jimmy; for Jimmy could get helpless enough to freeze in a drift on a dollar sixty-five.

"Oh, Jimmy, Jimmy!" muttered Dannie. "I wish ye wadna." And he was not thinking of himself, but of the eyes of the woman inside.

So Dannie did all the work, and cooked his supper, because he never ate in Jimmy's cabin when Jimmy was not there. Then he skinned rats, and watched the clock, because if Jimmy did not come by eleven, it meant he must drive to town and bring him home. No wonder Jimmy chilled at the trapping when he kept his blood on fire with whiskey. At half-past ten, Dannie, with scarcely half the rats finished, went out into the storm and hitched to the single buggy. Then he tapped at Mary Malone's door, quite softly, so that he would not disturb her if she had gone to bed. She was not sleeping, however, and the loneliness of her slight figure, as she stood with the lighted room behind her, struck Dannie forcibly, so that his voice trembled with pity as he said: "Mary, I've run out o' my curing compound juist in the midst of skinning the finest bunch o' rats we've taken frae the traps this winter. I am going to drive to town fra some more before the stores close, and we will be back in less than an hour. I thought I'd tell ye, so if ye wanted me ye wad know why I dinna answer. Ye winna be afraid, will ye?"

"No," replied Mary, "I won't be afraid."

"Bolt the doors, and pile on plenty of wood to keep ye warm," said Dannie as he turned away.

Just for a minute Mary stared out into the storm. Then a gust of wind nearly swept her from her feet, and she pushed the door shut, and slid the heavy bolt into place. For a little while she leaned and listened to the storm outside. She was a clean, neat, beautiful Irish woman. Her eyes were wide and blue, her cheeks pink, and her hair black and softly curling about her face and neck. The room in which she stood was neat as its keeper. The walls were whitewashed, and covered with prints, pictures, and some small tanned skins. Dried grasses and flowers filled the vases on the mantle. The floor was neatly carpeted with a striped rag carpet, and in the big open fireplace a wood fire roared. In an opposite corner stood a modern cooking stove, the pipe passing through a hole in the wall, and a door led into a sleeping room beyond.

As her eyes swept the room they rested finally on a framed lithograph of the Virgin, with the Infant in her arms. Slowly Mary advanced, her gaze fast on the serene pictured face of the mother clasping her child. Before it she stood staring. Suddenly her breast began to heave, and the big tears brimmed from her eyes and slid down her cheeks.

"Since you look so wise, why don't you tell me why?" she demanded. "Oh, if you have any mercy, tell me why!"

Then before the steady look in the calm eyes, she hastily made the sign of the cross, and slipping to the floor, she laid her head on a chair, and sobbed aloud.

Chapter II

RUBEN O'KHAYAM AND THE MILK PAIL

JIMMY Malone, carrying a shinning tin milk pail, stepped into Casey's saloon and closed the door behind him.

"E' much as wine has played the Infidel,
And robbed me of my robe of Honor—well,
I wonder what the Vinters buy
One-half so precious as the stuff they sell."

Jimmy stared at the back of a man leaning against the bar, and gazing lovingly at a glass of red wine, as he recited in mellow, swinging tones. Gripping the milk pail, Jimmy advanced a step. The man stuck a thumb in the belt of his Norfolk jacket, and the verses flowed on:

"The grape that can with logic absolute
The two and seventy jarring sects confute:
The sovereign Alchemist that in a trice
Life's leaden metal into Gold transmute."

Jimmy's mouth fell open, and he slowly nodded indorsement of the sentiment. The man lifted his glass.

"Ah, make the most of what we yet may spend,
Before we too into the Dust descend;
Yesterday this Day's Madness did prepare;
To-morrow's Silence, Triumph, or Despair:
Drink! for you know not whence you came nor why
Drink! for you know not why you go nor where."

Jimmy set the milk pail on the bar and faced the man.

"'Fore God, that's the only sensible word I ever heard on my side of the quistion in all me life. And to think that it should come from the mouth of a man wearing such a Go-to-Hell coat!"

Jimmy shoved the milk pail in front of the stranger. "In the name of humanity, impty yourself of that," he said. "Fill me pail with the stuff and let me take it home to Mary. She's always got the bist of the argumint, but I'm thinkin' that would cork her. You won't?" questioned Jimmy resentfully. "Kape it to yoursilf, thin, like you did your wine." He shoved the bucket toward the barkeeper, and emptied his pocket on the bar. "There, Casey, you be the Sovereign Alchemist, and transmute that metal into Melwood pretty quick, for I've not wet me whistle in three days, and the belly of me is filled with burnin' autumn leaves. Gimme a loving cup, and come on boys, this is on me while it lasts."

The barkeeper swept the coin into the till, picked up the bucket, and started back toward a beer keg.

"Oh, no you don't!" cried Jimmy. "Come back here and count that 'leaden metal,' and then be transmutin' it into whiskey straight, the purest gold you got. You don't drown out a three-days' thirst with beer. You ought to give me 'most two quarts for that."

The barkeeper was wise. He knew that what Jimmy started would go on with men who could pay, and he filled the order generously.

Jimmy picked up the pail. He dipped a small glass in the liquor, and held near an ounce aloft.

"I wonder what the Vinters buy
One-half so precious as the stuff they sell?"

he quoted. "Down goes!" and he emptied the glass at a draft. Then he walked to the group at the stove, and began dipping a drink for each.

When Jimmy came to a gray-haired man, with a high forehead and an intellectual face, he whispered: "Take your full time, Cap. Who's the rhymin' inkybator?"

"Thread man, Boston," mouthed the Captain, as he reached for the glass with trembling fingers. Jimmy held on. "Do you know that stuff he's giving off?" The Captain nodded, and rose to his feet. He always declared he could feel it farther if he drank standing.

"What's his name?" whispered Jimmy, releasing the glass. "Rubaiyat, Omar Khayyam," panted the Captain, and was lost. Jimmy finished the round of his friends, and then approached the bar.

His voice was softening. "Mister Ruben O'Khayam," he said, "it's me private opinion that ye nade lace-trimmed pantalettes and a sash to complate your costume, but barrin' clothes, I'm entangled in the thrid of your discourse. Bein' a Boston man meself, it appeals to me, that I detict the refinemint of the East in yer voice. Now these, me frinds, that I've just been tratin', are men of these parts; but we of the middle East don't set up to equal the culture of the extreme East. So, Mr. O'Khayam, solely for the benefit you might be to us, I'm askin' you to join me and me frinds in the momenchous initiation of me new milk pail."

Jimmy lifted a brimming glass, and offered it to the Thread Man. "Do you transmute?" he asked. Now if the Boston man had looked Jimmy in the eye, and said "I do," this book would not have been written. But he did not. He looked at the milk pail, and the glass, which had passed through the hands of a dozen men in a little country saloon away out in the wilds of Indiana, and said: "I do not care to partake of further refreshment; if I can be of intellectual benefit, I might remain for a time."

For a flash Jimmy lifted the five feet ten of his height to six; but in another he shrank below normal. What appeared to the Thread Man to be a humble, deferential seeker after wisdom, led him to one of the chairs around the big coal base burner. But the boys who knew Jimmy were watching the whites of his eyes, as they drank the second round. At this stage Jimmy was on velvet. How long he remained there depended on the depth of Melwood in the milk pail between his knees. He smiled winningly on the Thread Man.

"Ye know, Mister O'Khayam," he said, "at the present time you are located in one of the wooliest parts of the wild East. I don't suppose anything woolier could be found on the plains of Nebraska where I am reliably informed they've stuck up a pole and labeled it the cinter of the United States. Being a thousand miles closer that pole than you are in Boston, naturally we come by that distance closer to the great wool industry. Most of our wool here grows on our tongues, and we shear it by this transmutin' process, concerning which you have discoursed so beautiful. But barrin' the shearin' of our wool, we are the mildest, most sheepish fellows you could imagine. I don't reckon now there is a man among us who could be induced to blat or to butt, under the most tryin' circumstances. My Mary's got a little lamb, and all the rist of the boys are lambs. But all the lambs are waned, and clusterin' round the milk pail. Ain't that touchin'? Come on, now, Ruben, ile up and edify us some more!"

"On what point do you seek enlightenment?" inquired the Thread Man.

Jimmy stretched his long legs, and spat against the stove in pure delight.

"Oh, you might loosen up on the work of a man," he suggested. "These lambs of Casey's fold may larn things from you to help thim in the striss of life. Now here's Jones, for instance, he's holdin' togither a gang of sixty gibbering Atalyans; any wan of thim would cut his throat and skip in the night for a dollar, but he kapes the beast in thim under, and they're gettin' out gravel for the bed of a railway. Bingham there is oil. He's punchin' the earth full of wan thousand foot holes, and sendin' off two hundred quarts of nitroglycerine at the bottom of them, and pumpin' the accumulation across continents to furnish folks light and hate. York here is runnin' a field railway between Bluffton and Celina, so that I can get to the river and the resurvoir to fish without walkin'. Haines is bossin' a crew of forty Canadians and he's takin' the timber from the woods hereabouts, and sending it to be made into boats to carry stuff across sea. Meself, and me partner, Dannie Micnoun, are the lady-likest lambs in the bunch. We grow grub to feed folks in summer and trap for skins to cover 'em in winter. Corn is our great commodity. Plowin' and hoein' it in summer, and huskin' it in the fall is sich lamb-like work. But don't mintion it in the same brith with tendin' our four dozen fur traps on a twenty-below-zero day. Freezing hands and fate, and fallin' into air bubbles, and building fires to thaw out our frozen grub. Now here among us poor little, transmutin', lambs you come, a raging lion, ripresentin' the cultour and rayfinement of the far East. By the pleats on your breast you show us the style. By the thrid case in your hand you furnish us material so that our women can tuck their petticoats so fancy, and by the book in your head you teach us your sooperiority. By the same token, I wish I had that book in me head, for I could just squelch Dannie and Mary with it complate. Say, Mister O'Khayam, next time you come this way bring me a copy. I'm wantin' it bad. I got what you gave off all secure, but I take it there's more. No man goin' at that clip could shut off with thim few lines. Do you know the rist?"

The Thread Man knew the most of it, and although he was very uncomfortable, he did not know just how to get away, so he recited it. The milk pail was empty now, and Jimmy had almost forgotten that it was a milk pail, and seemed inclined to resent the fact that it had gone empty. He beat time on the bottom of it, and frequently interrupted the Thread Man to repeat a couplet which particularly suited him. By and by he got to his feet and began stepping off a slow dance to a sing-song repetition of lines that sounded musical to him, all the time marking the measures vigorously on the pail. When he tired of a couplet, he pounded the pail over the bar, stove, or chairs in encore, until the Thread Man could think up another to which he could dance.

"Wine! Wine! Wine! Red Wine!

The Nightingale cried to the rose,"

chanted Jimmy, thumping the pail in time, and stepping off the measures with feet that scarcely seemed to touch the floor. He flung his hat to the barkeeper, and his coat on a chair, ruffled his fingers through his thick auburn hair, and holding the pail under one arm, he paused, panting for breath and begging for more. The Thread Man sat on the edge of his chair, and the eyes he fastened on Jimmy were beginning to fill with interest.

> "Come fill the Cup and in the fire of Spring
> Your Winter-Garment of Repentance fling.
> The bird of time has but a little way to flutter
> And the bird is on the wing."

Smash came the milk pail across the bar. "Hooray!" shouted Jimmy. "Besht yet!" Bang! Bang! He was off." Bird ish on the wing," he chanted, and his feet flew. "Come fill the cup, and in the firesh of spring—Firesh of Spring, Bird ish on the Wing!" Between the music of the milk pail, the brogue of the panted verses, and the grace of Jimmy's flying feet, the Thread Man was almost prostrate. It suddenly came to him that here might be a chance to have a great time.

"More!" gasped Jimmy. "Me some more!" The Thread Man wiped his eyes.

> "Wether the cup with sweet or bitter run,
> The wine of life keeps oozing drop by drop,
> The leaves of life keep falling one by one."

Away went Jimmy.

> "Swate or bitter run,
> Laves of life kape falling one by one."

Bang! Bang! sounded a new improvision on the sadly battered pail, and to a new step Jimmy flashed back and forth the length of the saloon. At last he paused to rest a second. "One more! Just one more!" he begged.

"A Book of Verses underneath the Bough,
A jug of wine, a Loaf of Bread and Thou
Beside me singing in the Wilderness.
Oh, wilderness were Paradise enough!"

Jimmy's head dropped an instant. His feet slowly shuffled in improvising a new step, and then he moved away, thumping the milk pail and chanting:

"A couple of fish poles underneath a tree,
A bottle of Rye and Dannie beside me
A fishing in the Wabash.
Were the Wabash Paradise? HULLY GEE!

"Tired out, he dropped across a chair facing the back and folded his arms. He regained breath to ask the Thread Man: "Did you iver have a frind?"

He had reached the confidential stage.

The Boston man was struggling to regain his dignity. He retained the impression that at the wildest of the dance he had yelled and patted time for Jimmy.

"I hope I have a host of friends," he said, settling his pleated coat.

"Damn hosht!" said Jimmy. "Jisht in way. Now I got one frind, hosht all by himself. Be here pretty soon now. Alwaysh comesh nights like thish."

"Comes here?" inquired the Thread Man. "Am I to meet another interesting character?"

"Yesh, comesh here. Comesh after me. Comesh like the clock sthriking twelve. Don't he, boys?" inquired Jimmy. "But he ain't no interesting character. Jisht common man, Dannie is. Honest man. Never told a lie in his life. Yesh, he did, too. I forgot. He liesh for me. Jish liesh and liesh. Liesh to Mary. Tells her any old liesh to keep me out of schrape. You ever have frind hish up and drive ten milesh for you night like thish, and liesh to get you out of schrape?"

"I never needed any one to lie and get me out of a scrape," answered the Thread Man.

Jimmy sat straight and solemnly batted his eyes. "Gee! You musht misshed mosht the fun!" he said. "Me, I ain't ever misshed any. Always in schrape. But Dannie getsh me out. Good old Dannie. Jish like dog. Take care me all me life. See? Old folks come on same boat. Women get thick. Shettle beside. Build cabinsh together. Work together, and domn if they didn't get shmall pox and die together. Left me and Dannie. So we work together jish shame, and we fallsh in love with the shame girl. Dannie too slow. I got her." Jimmy wiped away great tears.

"How did you get her, Jimmy?" asked a man who remembered a story.

"How the nation did I get her?" Jimmy scratched his head, and appealed to the Thread Man. "Dannie besht man. Milesh besht man! Never lie—'cept for me. Never drink—'cept for me. Alwaysh save his money—'cept for me. Milesh besht man! Isn't he besht man, Spooley?"

"Ain't it true that you served Dannie a mean little trick?" asked the man who remembered.

Jimmy wasn't quite drunk enough, and the violent exercise of the dance somewhat sobered him. He glared at the man. "Whatsh you talkin' about?" he demanded.

"I'm just asking you," said the man, "why, if you played straight with Dannie about the girl, you never have had the face to go to confession since you married her."

"Alwaysh send my wife," said Jimmy grandly. "Domsh any woman that can't confiss enough for two!"

Then he hitched his chair closer to the Thread Man, and grew more confidential. "Shee here," he said. "Firsht I see your pleated coat, didn't like. But head's all right. Great head! Sthuck on frillsh there! Want to be let in on something? Got enough city, clubsh, an' all that? Want to taste real thing? Lesh go coon huntin'. Theysh tree down Canoper, jish short pleashant walk, got fify coons in it! Nobody knowsh the tree but me, shee? Been good to ush boys. Sat on same kind of chairs we do. Educate ush up lot. Know mosht that poetry till I die, shee? 'Wonner wash vinters buy, halfsh precious ash sthuff shell,' shee? I got it! Let you in on real thing. Take grand big coon skinch back to Boston with you. Ringsh on tail. Make wife fine muff, or fur trimmingsh. Good to till boysh at club about, shee?"

"Are you asking me to go on a coon hunt with you?" demanded the Thread Man. "When? Where?"

"Corshally invited," answered Jimmy. "To-morrow night. Canoper. Show you plashe. Bill Duke's dogs. My gunsh. Moonsh shinin'. Dogs howlin'. Shnow flying! Fify coonsh rollin' out one hole! Shoot all dead! Take your pick! Tan skin for you myself! Roaring big firesh warm by. Bag finesh sandwiches ever tasted. Milk pail pure gold drink. No stop, slop out going over bridge. Take jug. Big jug. Toss her up an' let her gurgle. Dogsh bark. Fire pop. Guns bang. Fifty coons drop. Boysh all go. Want to get more education. Takes culture to get woolsh off. Shay, will you go? "

"I wouldn't miss it for a thousand dollars," said the Thread Man. "But what will I say to my house for being a day late?"

"Shay gotter grip," suggested Jimmy. "Never too late to getter grip. Will you all go, boysh?"

There were not three men in the saloon who knew of a tree that had contained a coon that winter, but Jimmy was Jimmy, and to be trusted for an expedition of that sort; and all of them agreed to be at the saloon ready for the hunt at nine o'clock the next night. The Thread Man felt that he was going to see Life. He immediately invited the boys to the bar to drink to the success of the hunt.

"You shoot own coon yourself," offered the magnanimous Jimmy. "You may carrysh my gunsh, take first shot. First shot to Missher O'Khayam, boysh, 'member that. Shay, can you hit anything? Take a try now." Jimmy reached behind him, and shoved a big revolver into the hand of the Thread Man.

"Whersh target?" he demanded.

As he turned from the bar, the milk pail which he still carried under his arm caught on an iron rod. Jimmy gave it a jerk, and ripped the rim from the bottom. "Thish do," he said. "Splendid marksh. Shinesh jish like coon's eyesh in torch light."

He carried the pail to the back wall and hung it over a nail. The nail was straight, and the pail flaring. The pail fell. Jimmy kicked it across the room, and then gathered it up, and drove a dent in it with his heel that would hold over the nail. Then he went back to the Thread Man." Theresh mark, Ruben. Blash away!" he said.

The Boston man hesitated. "Whatsh the matter? Cansh shoot off nothing but your mouth?" demanded Jimmy. He caught the revolver and fired three shots so rapidly that the sounds came almost as one. Two bullets pierced the bottom of the pail, and the other the side as it fell.

The door opened, and with the rush of cold air Jimmy gave just one glance toward it, and slid the revolver into his pocket, reached for his hat, and started in the direction of his coat. "Glad to see you, Micnoun," he said. "If you are goingsh home, I'll jish ride out with you. Good night, boysh. Don't forgetsh the coon hunt," and Jimmy was gone.

A minute later the door opened again, and this time a man of nearly forty stepped inside. He had a manly form, and a manly face, was above the average in looks, and spoke with a slight Scotch accent.

"Do any of ye boys happen to know what it was Jimmy had with him when he came in here?"

A roar of laughter greeted the query. The Thread Man picked up the pail. As he handed it to Dannie, he said: "Mr. Malone said he was initiating a new milk pail, but I am afraid he has overdone the job."

"Thank ye," said Dannie, and taking the battered thing, he went out into the night.

Jimmy was asleep when he reached the buggy. Dannie had long since found it convenient to have no fence about his dooryard. He drove to the door, dragged Jimmy from the buggy, and stabled the horse. By hard work he removed Jimmy's coat and boots, laid him across the bed, and covered him. Then he grimly looked at the light in the next cabin. "Why doesna she go to bed?" he said. He summoned courage, and crossing the space between the two buildings, he tapped on the window. "It's me, Mary," he called. "The skins are only half done, and Jimmy is going to help me finish. He will come over in the morning. Ye go to bed. Ye needna be afraid. We will hear ye if ye even snore." There was no answer, but by a movement in the cabin Dannie knew that Mary was still dressed and waiting. He started back, but for an instant, heedless of the scurrying snow and biting cold, he faced the sky.

"I wonder if ye have na found a glib tongue and light feet the least part o' matrimony," he said. "Why in God's name couldna ye have married me? I'd like to know why."

As he closed the door, the cold air roused Jimmy.

"Dannie," he said, "donsh forget the milk pail. All 'niciate good now."

Chapter III

THE FIFTY COONS OF THE CANOPER

NEAR noon of the next day, Jimmy opened his eyes and stretched himself on Dannie's bed. It did not occur to him that he was sprawled across it in such a fashion that if Dannie had any sleep that night, he had taken it on chairs before the fireplace. At first Jimmy decided that he had a head on him, and would turn over and go back where he came from. Then he thought of the coon hunt, and sitting on the edge of the bed he laughed, as he looked about for his boots.

"I am glad ye are feeling so fine," said Dannie at the door, in a relieved voice. "I had a notion that ye wad be crosser than a badger when ye came to."

Jimmy laughed on.

"What's the fun?" inquired Dannie.

Jimmy thought hard a minute. Here was one instance where the truth would serve better than any invention, so he virtuously told Dannie all about it. Dannie thought of the lonely little woman next door, and rebelled.

"But, Jimmy!" he cried, "ye canna be gone all nicht again. It's too lonely fra Mary, and there's always a chance I might sleep sound and wadna hear if she should be sick or need ye."

"Then she can just yell louder, or come after you, or get well, for I am going, see? He was a thrid peddler in a dinky little pleated coat, Dannie. He laid up against the counter with his feet crossed at a dancing-girl angle. But I will say for him that he was running at the mouth with the finest flow of language I iver heard. I learned a lot of it, and Cap knows the stuff, and I'm goin' to have him get you the book. But, Dannie, he wouldn't drink with us, but he stayed to iducate us up a little. That little spool man, Dannie, iducatin' Jones of the gravel gang, and Bingham of the Standard, and York of the 'lectric railway, and Haines of the timber gang, not to mintion the champeen rat-catcher of the Wabash."

Jimmy hugged himself, and rocked on the edge of the bed.

"Oh, I can just see it, Dannie," he cried. "I can just see it now! I was pretty drunk, but I wasn't too drunk to think of it, and it came to me sudden like."

Dannie stared at Jimmy wide-eyed, while he explained the details, and then he too began to laugh, and the longer he laughed the funnier it grew.

"I've got to start," said Jimmy. "I've an awful afternoon's work. I must find him some rubber boots. He's to have the inestimable privilege of carryin' me gun, Dannie, and have the first shot at the coons, fifty, I'm thinkin' I said. And if I don't put some frills on his cute little coat! Oh, Dannie, it will break the heart of me if he don't wear that pleated coat!"

Dannie wiped his eyes.

"Come on to the kitchen," he said, "I've something ready fra ye to eat. Wash, while I dish it."

"I wish to Heaven you were a woman, Dannie," said Jimmy. "A fellow could fall in love with you, and marry you with some satisfaction. Crimminy, but I'm hungry!"

Jimmy ate greedily, and Dannie stepped about setting the cabin to rights. It lacked many feminine touches that distinguished Jimmy's as the abode of a woman; but it was neat and clean, and there seemed to be a place where everything belonged.

"Now, I'm off," said Jimmy, rising. "I'll take your gun, because I ain't goin' to see Mary till I get back."

"Oh, Jimmy, dinna do that!" pleaded Dannie. "I want my gun. Go and get your own, and tell her where ye are going and what ye are going to do. She'd feel less lonely."

"I know how she would feel better than you do," retorted Jimmy. "I am not going. If you won't give me your gun, I'll borrow one; or have all my fun spoiled."

Dannie took down the shining gun and passed it over. Jimmy instantly relented. He smiled an old boyish smile, that always caught Dannie in his softest spot.

"You are the bist frind I have on earth, Dannie," he said winsomely. "You are a man worth tying to. By gum, there's NOTHING I wouldn't do for you! Now go on, like the good fellow you are, and fix it up with Mary."

So Dannie started for the wood pile. In summer he could stand outside and speak through the screen. In winter he had to enter the cabin for errands like this, and as Jimmy's wood box was as heavily weighted on his mind as his own, there was nothing unnatural in his stamping snow on Jimmy's back stoop, and calling "Open!" to Mary at any hour of the day he happened to be passing the wood pile.

He stood at a distance, and patiently waited until a gray and black nut-hatch that foraged on the wood covered all the new territory discovered by the last disturbance of the pile. From loosened bark Dannie watched the bird take several good-sized white worms and a few dormant ants. As it flew away he gathered an armload of wood. He was very careful to clean his feet on the stoop, place the wood without tearing the neat covering of wall paper, and brush from his coat the snow and moss so that it fell in the box. He had heard Mary tell the careless Jimmy to do all these things, and Dannie knew that they saved her work. There was a whiteness on her face that morning that startled him, and long after the last particle of moss was cleaned from his sleeve he bent over the box trying to get something said. The cleaning took such a length of time that the glint of a smile crept into the grave eyes of the woman, and the grim line of her lips softened.

"Don't be feeling so badly about it, Dannie," she said. "I could have told you when you went after him last night that he would go back as soon as he wakened to-day. I know he is gone. I watched him lave."

Dannie brushed the other sleeve, on which there had been nothing at the start, and answered: "Noo, dinna ye misjudge him, Mary. He's goin' to a coon hunt to-nicht. Dinna ye see him take my gun?"

This evidence so bolstered Dannie that he faced Mary with confidence.

"There's a traveling man frae Boston in town, Mary, and he was edifying the boys a little, and Jimmy dinna like it. He's going to show him a little country sport to-nicht to edify him."

Dannie outlined the plan of Jimmy's campaign. Despite disapproval, and a sore heart, Mary Malone had to smile—perhaps as much over Dannie's eagerness in telling what was contemplated as anything.

"Why don't you take Jimmy's gun and go yoursilf?" she asked. "You haven't had a day off since fishing was over."

"But I have the work to do," replied Dannie, "and I couldna leave—" He broke off abruptly, but the woman supplied the word.

"Why can't you lave me, if Jimmy can? I'm not afraid. The snow and the cold will furnish me protiction to-night. There'll be no one to fear. Why should you do Jimmy's work, and miss the sport, to guard the thing he holds so lightly?"

The red flushed Dannie's cheeks. Mary never before had spoken like that. He had to say something for Jimmy quickly, and quickness was not his forte. His lips opened, but nothing came; for as Jimmy had boasted, Dannie never lied, except for him, and at those times he had careful preparation before he faced Mary. Now, he was overtaken unawares. He looked so boyish in his confusion, the mother in Mary's heart was touched.

"I'll till you what we'll do, Dannie," she said. "You tind the stock, and get in wood enough so that things won't be frazin' here; and then you hitch up and I'll go with you to town, and stay all night with Mrs. Dolan. You can put the horse in my sister's stable, and whin you and Jimmy get back, you'll be tired enough that you'll be glad to ride home. A visit with Katie will be good for me; I have been blue the last few days, and I can see you are just aching to go with the boys. Isn't that a fine plan?"

"I should say that IS a guid plan," answered the delighted Dannie. Anything to save Mary another night alone was good, and then—that coon hunt did sound alluring.

And that was how it happened that at nine o'clock that night, just as arrangements were being completed at Casey's, Dannie Macnoun stepped into the group and said to the astonished Jimmy: "Mary wanted to come to her sister's over nicht, so I fixed everything, and I'm going to the coon hunt, too, if you boys want me."

The crowd closed around Dannie, patted his back and cheered him, and he was introduced to Mister O'Khayam, of Boston, who tried to drown the clamor enough to tell what his name really was, "in case of accident"; but he couldn't be heard for Jimmy yelling that a good old Irish name like O'Khayam couldn't be beat in case of anything. And Dannie took a hasty glance at the Thread Man, to see if he wore that hated pleated coat, which lay at the bottom of Jimmy's anger.

Then they started. Casey's wife was to be left in charge of the saloon, and the Thread Man half angered Casey by a whispered conversation with her in a corner. Jimmy cut his crowd as low as he possibly could, but it numbered fifteen men, and no one counted the dogs. Jimmy led the way, the Thread Man beside him, and the crowd followed. The walking would be best to follow the railroad to the Canoper, and also they could cross the railroad bridge over the river and save quite a distance.

Jimmy helped the Thread Man into a borrowed overcoat and mittens, and loaded him with a twelve-pound gun, and they started. Jimmy carried a torch, and as torch bearer he was a rank failure, for he had a careless way of turning it and flashing it into people's faces that compelled them to jump to save themselves. Where the track lay clear and straight ahead the torch seemed to light it like day; but in dark places it was suddenly lowered or wavering somewhere else. It was through this carelessness of Jimmy's that at the first cattle-guard north of the village the torch flickered backward, ostensibly to locate Dannie, and the Thread Man went crashing down between the iron bars, and across the gun. Instantly Jimmy sprawled on top of him, and the next two men followed suit. The torch plowed into the snow and went out, and the yells of Jimmy alarmed the adjoining village.

He was hurt the worst of all, and the busiest getting in marching order again. "Howly smoke!" he panted. "I was havin' the time of me life, and plum forgot that cow-kitcher. Thought it was a quarter of a mile away yet. And liked to killed meself with me carelessness. But that's always the way in true sport. You got to take the knocks with the fun." No one asked the Thread Man if he was hurt, and he did not like to seem unmanly by mentioning a skinned shin, when Jimmy Malone seemed to have bursted most of his inside; so he shouldered his gun and limped along, now slightly in the rear of Jimmy. The river bridge was a serious matter with its icy coat, and danger of specials, and the torches suddenly flashed out from all sides; and the Thread Man gave thanks for Dannie Macnoun, who reached him a steady hand across the ties. The walk was three miles, and the railroad lay at from twenty to thirty feet elevation along the river and through the bottom land. The Boston man would have been thankful for the light, but as the last man stepped from the ties of the bridge all the torches went out save one. Jimmy explained they simply had to save them so that they could see where the coon fell when they began to shake the coon tree.

Just beside the water tank, and where the embankment was twenty feet sheer, Jimmy was cautioning the Boston man to look out, when the hunter next behind him gave a wild yell and plunged into his back. Jimmy's grab for him seemed more a push than a pull, and the three rolled to the bottom, and half way across the flooded ditch. The ditch was frozen over, but they were shaken, and smothered in snow. The whole howling party came streaming down the embankment. Dannie held aloft his torch and discovered Jimmy lying face down in a drift, making no effort to rise, and the Thread Man feebly tugging at him and imploring some one to come and help get Malone out. Then Dannie slunk behind the others and yelled until he was tired.

By and by Jimmy allowed himself to be dragged out.

"Who the thunder was that come buttin' into us?" he blustered. "I don't allow no man to butt into me when I'm on an imbankmint. Send the fool back here till I kill him."

The Thread Man was pulling at Jimmy's arm. "Don't mind, Jimmy," he gasped. "It was an accident! The man slipped. This is an awful place. I will be glad when we reach the woods. I'll feel safer with ground that's holding up trees under my feet. Come on, now! Are we not almost there? Should we not keep quiet from now on? Will we not alarm the coons?"

"Sure," said Jimmy. "Boys, don't hollo so much. Every blamed coon will be scared out of its hollow!"

"Amazing!" said the Thread Man. "How clever! Came on the spur of the moment. I must remember that to tell the Club. Do not hollo. Scare the coon out of its hollow!"

"Oh, I do miles of things like that," said Jimmy dryly, "and mostly I have to do thim before the spur of the moment; because our moments go so domn fast out here mighty few of thim have time to grow their spurs before they are gone. Here's where we turn. Now, boys, they've been trying to get this biler across the tracks here, and they've broke the ice. The water in this ditch is three feet deep and freezing cold. They've stuck getting the biler over, but I wonder if we can't cross on it, and hit the wood beyond. Maybe we can walk it."

Jimmy set a foot on the ice-covered boiler, howled, and fell back on the men behind him. "Jimminy crickets, we niver can do that!" he yelled. "It's a glare of ice and roundin'. Let's crawl through it! The rist of you can get through if I can. We'd better take off our overcoats, to make us smaller. We can roll thim into a bundle, and the last man can pull it through behind him."

Jimmy threw off his coat and entered the wrecked oil engine. He knew how to hobble through on his toes, but the pleated coat of the Boston man, who tried to pass through by stooping, got almost all Jimmy had in store for it. Jimmy came out all right with a shout. The Thread Man did not step half so far, and landed knee deep in the icy oil-covered slush of the ditch. That threw him off his balance, and Jimmy let him sink one arm in the pool, and then grabbed him, and scooped oil on his back with the other hand as he pulled. During the excitement and struggles of Jimmy and the Thread Man, the rest of the party jumped the ditch and gathered about, rubbing soot and oil on the Boston man, and he did not see how they crossed.

Jimmy continued to rub oil and soot into the hated coat industriously. The dogs leaped the ditch, and the instant they struck the woods broke away baying over fresh tracks. The men yelled like mad. Jimmy struggled into his overcoat, and helped the almost insane Boston man into his and then they hurried after the dogs.

The scent was so new and clear the dogs simply raged. The Thread Man was wild, Jimmy was wilder, and the thirteen contributed all they could for laughing. Dannie forgot to be ashamed of himself and followed the example of the crowd. Deeper and deeper into the wild, swampy Canoper led the chase. With a man on either side to guide him into the deepest holes and to shove him into bushy thickets, the skinned, soot-covered, oil-coated Boston man toiled and sweated. He had no time to think, the excitement was so intense. He scrambled out of each pitfall set for him, and plunged into the next with such uncomplaining bravery that Dannie very shortly grew ashamed, and crowding up beside him he took the heavy gun and tried to protect him all he could without falling under the eye of Jimmy, who was keeping close watch on the Boston man.

Wild yelling told that the dogs had treed, and with shaking fingers the Thread Man pulled off the big mittens he wore and tried to lift the gun. Jimmy flashed a torch, and sure enough, in the top of a medium hickory tree, the light was reflected in streams from the big shining eyes of a coon. "Treed!" yelled Jimmy frantically. "Treed! and big as an elephant. Company's first shot. Here, Mister O'Khayam, here's a good place to stand. Gee, what luck! Coon in sight first thing, and Mellen's food coon at that! Shoot, Mister O'Khayam, shoot!"

The Thread Man lifted the wavering gun, but it was no use.

"Tell you what, Ruben," said Jimmy. "You are too tired to shoot straight. Let's take a rist, and ate our lunch. Then we'll cut down the tree and let the dogs get cooney. That way there won't be any shot marks in his skin. What do you say? Is that a good plan?"

They all said that was the proper course, so they built a fire, and placed the Thread Man where he could see the gleaming eyes of the frightened coon, and where all of them could feast on his soot and oil-covered face. Then they opened the bag and passed the sandwiches.

"I really am hungry," said the weary Thread Man, biting into his with great relish. His jaws moved once or twice experimentally, and then he lifted his handkerchief to his lips.

"I wish 'twas as big as me head," said Jimmy, taking a great bite, and then he began to curse uproariously.

"What ails the things?" inquired Dannie, ejecting a mouthful. And then all of them began to spit birdshot, and started an inquest simultaneously. Jimmy raged. He swore some enemy had secured the bag and mined the feast; but the boys who knew him laughed until it seemed the Thread Man must suspect. He indignantly declared it was a dirty trick. By the light of the fire he knelt and tried to free one of the sandwiches from its sprinkling of birdshot, so that it would be fit for poor Jimmy, who had worked so hard to lead them there and tree the coon. For the first time Jimmy looked thoughtful.

But the sight of the Thread Man was too much for him, and a second later he was thrusting an ax into the hands accustomed to handling a thread case. Then he led the way to the tree, and began chopping at the green hickory. It was slow work, and soon the perspiration streamed. Jimmy pulled off his coat and threw it aside. He assisted the Thread Man out of his and tossed it behind him. The coat alighted in the fire, and was badly scorched before it was rescued. But the Thread Man was game. Fifty times that night it had been said that he was to have the first coon, of course he should work for it. So with the ax with which Casey chopped ice for his refrigerator, the Boston man banged against the hickory, and swore to himself because he could not make the chips fly as Jimmy did.

"Iverybody clear out!" cried Jimmy. "Number one is coming down. Get the coffee sack ready. Baste cooney over the head and shove him in before the dogs tear the skin. We want a dandy big pelt out of this!"

There was a crack, and the tree fell with a crash. All the Boston man could see was that from a tumbled pile of branches, dogs, and men, some one at last stepped back, gripping a sack, and cried: "Got it all right, and it's a buster."

"Now for the other forty-nine!" shouted Jimmy, straining into his coat.

"Come on, boys, we must secure a coon for every one," cried the Thread Man, heartily as any member of the party might have said it. But the rest of the boys suddenly grew tired. They did not want any coons, and after some persuasion the party agreed to go back to Casey's to warm up. The Thread Man got into his scorched, besooted, oil-smeared coat, and the overcoat which had been loaned him, and shouldered the gun. Jimmy hesitated. But Dannie came up to the Boston man and said: "There's a place in my shoulder that gun juist fits, and it's lonesome without it. Pass it over." Only the sorely bruised and strained Thread Man knew how glad he was to let it go.

It was Dannie, too, who whispered to the Thread Man to keep close behind him; and when the party trudged back to Casey's it was so surprising how much better he knew the way going back than Jimmy had known it coming out, that the Thread Man did remark about it. But Jimmy explained that after one had been out a few hours their eyes became accustomed to the darkness and they could see better. That was reasonable, for the Thread Man knew it was true in his own experience.

So they got back to Casey's, and found a long table set, and a steaming big oyster supper ready for them; and that explained the Thread Man's conference with Mrs. Casey. He took the head of the table, with his back to the wall, and placed Jimmy on his right and Dannie on his left. Mrs. Casey had furnished soap and towels, and at least part of the Boston man's face was clean. The oysters were fine, and well cooked. The Thread Man recited more of the wonderful poem for Dannie's benefit, and told jokes and stories. They laughed until they were so weak they could only pound the table to indicate how funny it was. And at the close, just as they were making a movement to rise, Casey proposed that he bring in the coon, and let all of them get a good look at their night's work. The Thread Man applauded, and Casey brought in the bag and shook it bottom up over the floor. Therefrom there issued a poor, frightened, maltreated little pet coon of Mrs. Casey's, and it dexterously ran up Casey's trouser leg and hid its nose in his collar, its chain dragging behind. And that was so funny the boys doubled over the table, and laughed and screamed until a sudden movement brought them to their senses.

The Thread Man was on his feet, and his eyes were no laughing matter. He gripped his chair back, and leaned toward Jimmy. "You walked me into that cattle-guard on purpose!" he cried.

Silence.

"You led me into that boiler, and fixed the oil at the end!"

No answer.

"You mauled me all over the woods, and loaded those sandwiches yourself, and sored me for a week trying to chop down a tree with a pet coon chained in it! You——! You——! What had I done to you?"

"You wouldn't drink with me, and I didn't like the domned, dinky, little pleated coat you wore," answered Jimmy.

One instant amazement held sway on the Thread Man's face; the next, "And damned if I like yours!" he cried, and catching up a bowl half filled with broth he flung it squarely into Jimmy's face.

Jimmy, with a great oath, sprang at the Boston man. But once in his life Dannie was quick. For the only time on record he was ahead of Jimmy, and he caught the uplifted fist in a grip that Jimmy's use of whiskey and suffering from rheumatism had made his master.

"Steady—Jimmy, wait a minute," panted Dannie. "This mon is na even wi' ye yet. When every muscle in your body is strained, and every inch of it bruised, and ye are daubed wi' soot, and bedraggled in oil, and he's made ye the laughin' stock fra strangers by the hour, ye will be juist even, and ready to talk to him. Every minute of the nicht he's proved himself a mon, and right now he's showed he's na coward. It's up to ye, Jimmy. Do it royal. Be as much of a mon as he is. Say ye are sorry!"

One tense instant the two friends faced each other.

Then Jimmy's fist unclenched, and his arms dropped. Dannie stepped back, trying to breathe lightly, and it was between Jimmy and the Thread Man.

"I am sorry," said Jimmy. "I carried my objictions to your wardrobe too far. If you'll let me, I'll clean you up. If you'll take it, I'll raise you the price of a new coat, but I'll be domn if I'll hilp put such a man as you are into another of the fiminine ginder."

The Thread Man laughed, and shook Jimmy's hand; and then Jimmy proved why every one liked him by turning to Dannie and taking his hand. "Thank you, Dannie," he said. "You sure hilped me to mesilf that time. If I'd hit him, I couldn't have hild up me head in the morning."

Chapter IV

WHEN THE KINGFISHER AND THE BLACK BASS CAME HOME

"CRIMMINY, but you are slow." Jimmy made the statement, not as one voices a newly discovered fact, but as one iterates a time-worn truism. He sat on a girder of the Limberlost bridge, and scraped the black muck from his boots in a little heap. Then he twisted a stick into the top of his rat sack, preparatory to his walk home. The ice had broken on the river, and now the partners had to separate at the bridge, each following his own line of traps to the last one, and return to the bridge so that Jimmy could cross to reach home. Jimmy was always waiting, after the river opened, and it was a remarkable fact to him that as soon as the ice was gone his luck failed him. This evening the bag at his feet proved by its bulk that it contained just about one-half the rats Dannie carried.

"I must set my traps in my own way," answered Dannie calmly. "If I stuck them into the water ony way and went on, so would the rats. A trap is no a trap unless it is concealed."

"That's it! Go on and give me a sarmon!" urged Jimmy derisively. "Who's got the bulk of the rats all winter? The truth is that my side of the river is the best catching in the extrame cold, and you get the most after the thaws begin to come. The rats seem to have a lot of burrows and shift around among thim. One time I'm ahead, and the nixt day they go to you: But it don't mane that you are any better TRAPPER than I am. I only got siven to-night. That's a sweet day's work for a whole man. Fifteen cints apace for sivin rats. I've a big notion to cut the rat business, and compete with Rocky in ile."

Dannie laughed. "Let's hurry home, and get the skinning over before nicht," he said. "I think the days are growing a little longer. I seem to scent spring in the air to-day."

Jimmy looked at Dannie's mud-covered, wet clothing, his blood-stained mittens and coat back, and the dripping bag he had rested on the bridge. "I've got some music in me head, and some action in me feet," he said, "but I guess God forgot to put much sintimint into me heart. The breath of spring niver got so strong with me that I could smell it above a bag of muskrats and me trappin' clothes."

He arose, swung his bag to his shoulder, and together they left the bridge, and struck the road leading to Rainbow Bottom. It was late February. The air was raw, and the walking heavy. Jimmy saw little around him, and there was little Dannie did not see. To him, his farm, the river, and the cabins in Rainbow Bottom meant all there was of life, for all he loved on earth was there. But loafing in town on rainy days, when Dannie sat with a book; hearing the talk at Casey's, at the hotel, and on the streets, had given Jimmy different views of life, and made his lot seem paltry compared with that of men who had greater possessions. On days when Jimmy's luck was bad, or when a fever of thirst burned him, he usually discoursed on some sort of intangible experience that men had, which he called "seeing life." His rat bag was unusually light that night, and in a vague way he connected it with the breaking up of the ice. When the river lay solid he usually carried home just twice the rats Dannie had, and as he had patronized Dannie all his life, it fretted Jimmy to be behind even one day at the traps.

"Be Jasus, I get tired of this!" he said. "Always and foriver the same thing. I kape goin' this trail so much that I've got a speakin' acquaintance with meself. Some of these days I'm goin' to take a trip, and have a little change. I'd like to see Chicago, and as far west as the middle, anyway."

"Well, ye canna go," said Dannie. "Ye mind the time when ye were married, and I thought I'd be best away, and packed my trunk? When ye and Mary caught me, ye got mad as fire, and she cried, and I had to stay. Just ye try going, and I'll get mad, and Mary will cry, and ye will stay at home, juist like I did."

There was a fear deep in Dannie's soul that some day Jimmy would fulfill this long-time threat of his. "I dinna think there is ony place in all the world so guid as the place ye own," Dannie said earnestly. "I dinna care a penny what anybody else has, probably they have what they want. What *I* want is the land that my feyther owned before me, and the house that my mither kept. And they'll have to show me the place they call Eden before I'll give up that it beats Rainbow Bottom—Summer, Autumn, or Winter. I dinna give twa hoops fra the palaces men rig up, or the thing they call 'landscape gardening'. When did men ever compete with the work of God? All the men that have peopled the earth since time began could have their brains rolled into one, and he would stand helpless before the anatomy of one of the rats in these bags. The thing God does is guid enough fra me."

"Why don't you take a short cut to the matin'-house?" inquired Jimmy.

"Because I wad have nothing to say when I got there," retorted Dannie. "I've a meetin'-house of my ain, and it juist suits me; and I've a God, too, and whether He is spirit or essence, He suits me. I dinna want to be held to sharper account than He faces me up to, when I hold communion with mesel'. I dinna want any better meetin'-house than Rainbow Bottom. I dinna care for better talkin' than the 'tongues in the trees'; sounder preachin' than the 'sermons in the stones'; finer readin' than the books in the river; no, nor better music than the choir o' the birds, each singin' in its ain way fit to burst its leetle throat about the mate it won, the nest they built, and the babies they are raising. That's what I call the music o' God, spontaneous, and the soul o' joy. Give it me every time compared with notes frae a book. And all the fine places that the wealth o' men ever evolved winna begin to compare with the work o' God, and I've got that around me every day."

"But I want to see life," wailed Jimmy.

"Then open your eyes, mon, fra the love o' mercy, open your eyes! There's life sailing over your heid in that flock o' crows going home fra the night. Why dinna ye, or some other mon, fly like that? There's living roots, and seeds, and insects, and worms by the million wherever ye are setting foot. Why dinna ye creep into the earth and sleep through the winter, and renew your life with the spring? The trouble with ye, Jimmy, is that ye've always followed your heels. If ye'd stayed by the books, as I begged ye, there now would be that in your heid that would teach ye that the old story of the Rainbow is true. There is a pot of gold, of the purest gold ever smelted, at its foot, and we've been born, and own a good living richt there. An' the gold is there; that I know, wealth to shame any bilious millionaire, and both of us missing the pot when we hold the location. Ye've the first chance, mon, fra in your life is the great prize mine will forever lack. I canna get to the bottom of the pot, but I'm going to come close to it as I can; and as for ye, empty it! Take it all! It's yours! It's fra the mon who finds it, and we own the location."

"Aha! We own the location," repeated Jimmy. "I should say we do! Behold our hotbed of riches! I often lay awake nights thinkin' about my attachmint to the place.

> "How dear to me heart are the scanes of me childhood,
> Fondly gaze on the cabin where I'm doomed to dwell,
> Those chicken-coop, thim pig-pen, these highly piled-wood
> Around which I've always raised Hell."

Jimmy turned in at his own gate, while Dannie passed to the cabin beyond. He entered, set the dripping rat bag in a tub, raked open the buried fire and threw on a log. He always ate at Jimmy's when Jimmy was at home, so there was no supper to get. He went out to the barn, wading mud ankle deep, fed and bedded his horses, and then went over to Jimmy's barn, and completed his work up to milking. Jimmy came out with the pail, and a very large hole in the bottom of it was covered with dried dough. Jimmy looked at it disapprovingly.

"I bought a new milk pail the other night. I know I did," he said. "Mary was kicking for one a month ago, and I went after it the night I met Ruben O'Khayam. Now what the nation did I do with that pail?"

"I have wondered mysel'," answered Dannie, as he leaned over and lifted a strange looking object from a barrel. "This is what ye brought home, Jimmy."

Jimmy stared at the shining, battered, bullet-punctured pail in amazement. Slowly he turned it over and around, and then he lifted bewildered eyes to Dannie.

"Are you foolin'?" he asked. "Did I bring that thing home in that shape?"

"Honest!" said Dannie.

"I remember buyin' it," said Jimmy slowly. "I remember hanging on to it like grim death, for it was the wan excuse I had for goin', but I don't just know how—!" Slowly he revolved the pail, and then he rolled over in the hay and laughed until he was tired. Then he sat up and wiped his eyes. "Great day! What a lot of fun I must have had before I got that milk pail into that shape," he said. "Domned if I don't go straight to town and buy another one; yes, bedad! I'll buy two!"

In the meantime Dannie milked, fed and watered the cattle, and Jimmy picked up the pail of milk and carried it to the house. Dannie came by the wood pile and brought in a heavy load. Then they washed, and sat down to supper.

"Seems to me you look unusually perky," said Jimmy to his wife. "Had any good news?"

"Splendid!" said Mary. "I am so glad! And I don't belave you two stupids know!"

"You niver can tell by lookin' at me what I know," said Jimmy. "Whin I look the wisest I know the least. Whin I look like a fool, I'm thinkin' like a philosopher."

"Give it up," said Dannie promptly. You would not catch him knowing anything it would make Mary's eyes shine to tell.

"Sap is running!" announced Mary.

"The Divil you say!" cried Jimmy.

"It is!" beamed Mary. "It will be full in three days. Didn't you notice how green the maples are? I took a little walk down to the bottom to-day. I niver in all my life was so tired of winter, and the first thing I saw was that wet look on the maples, and on the low land, where they are sheltered and yet get the sun, several of them are oozing!"

"Grand!" cried Dannie. "Jimmy, we must peel those rats in a hurry, and then clean the spiles, and see how mony new ones we will need. To-morrow we must come frae the traps early and look up our troughs."

"Oh, for pity sake, don't pile up work enough to kill a horse," cried Jimmy. "Ain't you ever happy unless you are workin'?"

"Yes," said Dannie. "Sometimes I find a book that suits me, and sometimes the fish bite, and sometimes it's in the air."

"Git the condinser" said Jimmy. "And that reminds me, Mary, Dannie smelled spring in the air to-day."

"Well, what if he did?" questioned Mary. "I can always smell it. A little later, when the sap begins to run in all the trees, and the buds swell, and the ice breaks up, and the wild geese go over, I always scent spring; and when the catkins bloom, then it comes strong, and I just love it. Spring is my happiest time. I have more news, too!"

"Don't spring so much at wance!" cried Jimmy, "you'll spoil my appetite."

"I guess there's no danger," replied Mary.

"There is," said Jimmy. "At laste in the fore siction. 'Appe' is Frinch, and manes atin'. 'Tite' is Irish, and manes drinkin'. Appetite manes atin' and drinkin' togither. 'Tite' manes drinkin' without atin', see?"

"I was just goin' to mintion it meself," said Mary, "it's where you come in strong. There's no danger of anybody spoilin' your drinkin', if they could interfere with your atin'. You guess, Dannie."

"The dominick hen is setting," ventured Dannie, and Mary's face showed that he had blundered on the truth.

"She is," affirmed Mary, pouring the tea, "but it is real mane of you to guess it, when I've so few new things to tell. She has been setting two days, and she went over fifteen fresh eggs to-day. In just twenty-one days I will have fiftane the cunningest little chickens you ever saw, and there is more yet. I found the nest of the gray goose, and there are three big eggs in it, all buried in feathers. She must have stripped her breast almost bare to cover them. And I'm the happiest I've been all winter. I hate the long, lonely, shut-in time. I am going on a delightful spree. I shall help boil down sugar-water and make maple syrup. I shall set hins, and geese, and turkeys. I shall make soap, and clane house, and plant seed, and all my flowers will bloom again. Goody for summer; it can't come too soon to suit me."

"Lord! I don't see what there is in any of those things," said Jimmy. "I've got just one sign of spring that interests me. If you want to see me caper, somebody mention to me the first rattle of the Kingfisher. Whin he comes home, and house cleans in his tunnel in the embankment, and takes possession of his stump in the river, the nixt day the Black Bass locates in the deep water below the shoals. THIN you can count me in. There is where business begins for Jimmy boy. I am going to have that Bass this summer, if I don't plant an acre of corn."

"I bet you that's the truth!" said Mary, so quickly that both men laughed.

"Ahem!" said Dannie. "Then I will have to do my plowing by a heidlicht, so I can fish as much as ye do in the day time. I hereby make, enact, and enforce a law that neither of us is to fish in the Bass hole when the other is not there to fish also. That is the only fair way. I've as much richt to him as ye have."

"Of course!" said Mary. "That is a fair way. Make that a rule, and kape it. If you both fish at once, it's got to be a fair catch for the one that lands it; but whoever catches it, I shall ate it, so it don't much matter to me."

"You ate it!" howled Jimnmy. "I guess not. Not a taste of that fish, when he's teased me for years? He's as big as a whale. If Jonah had had the good fortune of falling in the Wabash, and being swallowed by the Black Bass, he could have ridden from Peru to Terre Haute, and suffered no inconvanience makin' a landin'. Siven pounds he'll weigh by the steelyard I'll wager you."

"Five, Jimmy, five," corrected Dannie.

"Siven!" shouted Jimmy. " Ain't I hooked him repeated? Ain't I seen him broadside? I wonder if thim domn lines of mine have gone and rotted."

He left his supper, carrying his chair, and standing on it he began rummaging the top shelf of the cupboard for his box of tackle. He knocked a bottle from the shelf, but caught it in mid-air with a dexterous sweep.

"Spirits are movin'," cried Jimmy, as he restored the camphor to its place. He carried the box to the window, and became so deeply engrossed in its contents that he did not notice when Dannie picked up his rat bag and told him to come on and help skin their day's catch. Mary tried to send him, and he was going in a minute, but the minute stretched and stretched, and both of them were surprised when the door opened and Dannie entered with an armload of spiles, and the rat-skinning was all over. So Jimmy went on unwinding lines, and sharpening hooks, and talking fish; while Dannie and Mary cleaned the spiles, and figured on how many new elders must be cut and prepared for more on the morrow; and planned the sugar making.

When it was bedtime, and Dannie had gone an Jimmy and Mary closed their cabin for the night, Mary stepped to the window that looked on Dannie's home to see if his light was burning. It was, and clear in its rays stood Dannie, stripping yard after yard of fine line through his fingers, and carefully examining it. Jimmy came and stood beside her as she wondered.

"Why, the domn son of the Rainbow," he cried, "if he ain't testing his fish lines!"

The next day Mary Malone was rejoicing when the men returned from trapping, and gathering and cleaning the sugar-water troughs. There had been a robin at the well.

"Kape your eye on, Mary" advised Jimmy. "If she ain't watched close from this time on, she'll be settin' hins in snowdrifts, and pouring biling water on the daffodils to sprout them."

On the first of March, five killdeers flew over in a flock, and a half hour later one straggler crying piteously followed in their wake.

"Oh, the mane things!" almost sobbed Mary. "Why don't they wait for it?"

She stood by a big kettle of boiling syrup at the sugar camp, almost helpless in Jimmy's boots and Dannie's great coat. Jimmy cut and carried wood, and Dannie hauled sap. All the woods were stirred by the smell of the curling smoke and the odor of the boiling sap, fine as the fragrance of flowers. Bright-eyed deer mice peeped at her from under old logs, the chickadees, nuthatches, and jays started an investigating committee to learn if anything interesting to them was occurring. One gayly-dressed little sapsucker hammered a tree near by and scolded vigorously.

"Right you are!" said Mary. "It's a pity you're not big enough to drive us from the woods, for into one kittle goes enough sap to last you a lifetime."

The squirrels were sure it was an intrusion, and raced among the branches overhead, barking loud defiance. At night the three rode home on the sled, with the syrup jugs beside them, and Mary's apron was filled with big green rolls of pungent woolly-dog moss.

Jimmy built the fires, Dannie fed the stock, and Mary cooked the supper. When it was over, while the men warmed chilled feet and fingers by the fire, Mary poured some syrup into a kettle, and just as it "sugared off" she dipped streams of the amber sweetness into cups of water. All of them ate it like big children, and oh, but it was good! Two days more of the same work ended sugar making, but for the next three days Dannie gathered the rapidly diminishing sap for the vinegar barrel.

Then there were more hens ready to set, water must be poured hourly into the ash hopper to start the flow of lye for soap making, and the smoke house must be gotten ready to cure the hams and pickled meats, so that they would keep during warm weather. The bluebells were pushing through the sod in a race with the Easter and star flowers. One morning Mary aroused Jimmy with a pull at his arm.

"Jimmy, Jimmy," she cried. "Wake up!"

"Do you mane, wake up, or get up?" asked Jimmy sleepily.

"Both," cried Mary. "The larks are here!"

A little later Jimmy shouted from the back door to the barn: "Dannie, do you hear the larks?"

"Ye bet I do," answered Dannie. "Heard ane goin' over in the nicht. How long is it now till the Kingfisher comes?"

"Just a little while," said Jimmy. "If only these March storms would let up 'stid of down! He can't come until he can fish, you know. He's got to have crabs and minnies to live on."

A few days later the green hylas began to pipe in the swamps, the bullfrogs drummed among the pools in the bottom, the doves cooed in the thickets, and the breath of spring was in the nostrils of all creation, for the wind was heavy with the pungent odor of catkin pollen. The spring flowers were two inches high. The peonies and rhubarb were pushing bright yellow and red cones through the earth. The old gander, leading his flock along the Wabash, had hailed passing flocks bound northward until he was hoarse; and the Brahma rooster had threshed the yellow dorkin until he took refuge under the pig pen, and dare not stick out his unprotected head.

The doors had stood open at supper time, and Dannie staid up late, mending and oiling the harness. Jimmy sat by cleaning his gun, for to his mortification he had that day missed killing a crow which stole from the ash hopper the egg with which Mary tested the strength of the lye. In a basket behind the kitchen stove fifteen newly hatched yellow chickens, with brown stripes on their backs, were peeping and nestling; and on wing the killdeers cried half the night. At two o'clock in the morning came a tap on the Malone's bedroom window.

"Dannie?" questioned Mary, half startled.

"Tell Jimmy!" cried Dannie's breathless voice outside. "Tell him the Kingfisher has juist struck the river!"

Jimmy sat straight up in bed.

"Then glory be!" he cried. "To-morrow the Black Bass comes home!"

Chapter V

WHEN THE RAINBOW SET ITS ARCH IN THE SKY

"WHERE did Jimmy go?" asked Mary.

Jimmy had been up in time to feed the chickens and carry in the milk, but he disappeared shortly after breakfast.

Dannie almost blushed as he answered: "He went to take a peep at the river. It's going down fast. When it gets into its regular channel, spawning will be over and the fish will come back to their old places. We figure that the Black Bass will be home to-day."

"When you go digging for bait," said Mary, "I wonder if the two of you could make it convanient to spade an onion bed. If I had it spaded I could stick the sets mesilf."

"Now, that amna fair, Mary," said Dannie. "We never went fishing till the garden was made, and the crops at least wouldna suffer. We'll make the beds, of course, juist as soon as they can be spaded, and plant the seed, too."

"I want to plant the seeds mesilf," said Mary.

"And we dinna want ye should," replied Dannie. "All we want ye to do, is to boss."

"But I'm going to do the planting mesilf," Mary was emphatic. "It will be good for me to be in the sunshine, and I do enjoy working in the dirt, so that for a little while I'm happy."

"If ye want to put the onions in the highest place, I should think I could spade ane bed now, and enough fra lettuce and radishes."

Dannie went after a spade, and Mary Malone laughed softly as she saw that he also carried an old tin can. He tested the earth in several places, and then called to her: "All right, Mary! Ground in prime shape. Turns up dry and mellow. We will have the garden started in no time."

He had spaded but a minute when Mary saw him run past the window, leap the fence, and go hurrying down the path to the river. She went to the door. At the head of the lane stood Jimmy, waving his hat, and the fresh morning air carried his cry clearly: "Gee, Dannie! Come hear him splash!"

Just why that cry, and the sight of Dannie Macnoun racing toward the river, his spade lying on the upturned earth of her scarcely begun onion bed, should have made her angry, it would be hard to explain. He had no tackle or bait, and reason easily could have told her that he would return shortly, and finish anything she wanted done; but when was a lonely, disappointed woman ever reasonable?

She set the dish water on the stove, wiped her hands on her apron, and walking to the garden, picked up the spade and began turning great pieces of earth. She had never done rough farm work, such as women all about her did; she had little exercise during the long, cold winter, and the first half dozen spadefuls tired her until the tears of self-pity rolled.

"I wish there was a turtle as big as a wash tub in the river" she sobbed, "and

I wish it would eat that old Black Bass to the last scale. And I'm going to take the shotgun, and go over to the embankment, and poke it into the tunnel, and blow the old Kingfisher through into the cornfield. Then maybe Dannie won't go off too and leave me. I want this onion bed spaded right away, so I do."

"Drop that! Idjit! What you doing?" yelled Jimmy.

"Mary, ye goose!" panted Dannie, as he came hurrying across the yard. "Wha' do ye mean? Ye knew I'd be back in a minute! Jimmy juist called me to hear the Bass splash. I was comin' back. Mary, this amna fair."

Dannie took the spade from her hand, and Mary fled sobbing to the house.

"What's the row?" demanded Jimmy of the suffering Dannie.

"I'd juist started spadin' this onion bed," explained Dannie. "Of course, she thought we were going to stay all day."

"With no poles, and no bait, and no grub? She didn't think any such a domn thing," said Jimmy. "You don't know women! She just got to the place where it's her time to spill brine, and raise a rumpus about something, and aisy brathin' would start her. Just let her bawl it out, and thin—we'll get something dacent for dinner."

Dannie turned a spadeful of earth and broke it open, and Jimmy squatted by the can, and began picking out the angle worms.

"I see where we dinna fish much this summer," said Dannie, as he waited. "And where we fish close home when we do, and where all the work is done before we go."

"Aha, borrow me rose-colored specks!" cried Jimmy. "I don't see anything but what I've always seen. I'll come and go as I please, and Mary can do the same. I don't throw no `jeminy fit' every time a woman acts the fool a little, and if you'd lived with one fiftane years you wouldn't either. Of course we'll make the garden. Wish to goodness it was a beer garden! Wouldn't I like to plant a lot of hop seed and see rows of little green beer bottles humpin' up the dirt. Oh, my! What all does she want done?"

Dannie turned another spadeful of earth and studied the premises, while Jimmy gathered the worms.

"Palins all on the fence?" asked Dannie.

"Yep," said Jimmy.

"Well, the yard is to be raked."

"Yep."

"The flooer beds spaded."

"Yep."

"Stones around the peonies, phlox, and hollyhocks raised and manure worked in. All the trees must be pruned, the bushes and vines trimmed, and the gooseberries, currants, and raspberries thinned. The strawberry bed must be fixed up, and the rhubarb and asparagus spaded around and manured. This whole garden must be made——"

"And the road swept, and the gate sandpapered, and the barn whitewashed! Return to grazing, Nebuchadnezzar," said Jimmy. "We do what's raisonable, and then we go fishin'. See?"

Three beds spaded, squared, and ready for seeding lay in the warm spring sunshine before noon. Jimmy raked the yard, and Dannie trimmed the gooseberries. Then he wheeled a barrel of swamp loam for a flower bed by the cabin wall, and listened intently between each shovelful he threw. He could not hear a sound. What was more, he could not bear it. He went to Jimmy.

"Say, Jimmy," he said. "Dinna ye have to gae in fra a drink?"

"House or town?" inquired Jimmy sweetly.

"The house!" exploded Dannie. "I dinna hear a sound yet. Ye gae in fra a drink, and tell Mary I want to know where she'd like the new flooer bed she's been talking about."

Jimmy leaned the rake against a tree, and started.

"And Jimmy," said Dannie. "If she's quit crying, ask her what was the matter. I want to know."

Jimmy vanished. Presently he passed Dannie where he worked.

"Come on," whispered Jimmy.

The bewildered Dannie followed. Jimmy passed the wood pile, and pig pen, and slunk around behind the barn, where he leaned against the logs and held his sides. Dannie stared at him.

"She says," wheezed Jimmy, "that she guesses SHE wanted to go and hear the Bass splash, too!"

Dannie's mouth fell open, and then closed with a snap.

"Us fra the fool killer!" he said. "Ye dinna let her see ye laugh?"

"Let her see me laugh!" cried Jimmy. "Let her see me laugh! I told her she wasn't to go for a few days yet, because we were sawin' the Kingfisher's stump up into a rustic sate for her, and we were goin' to carry her out to it, and she was to sit there and sew, and umpire the fishin', and whichiver bait she told the Bass to take, that one of us would be gettin' it. And she was pleased as anything, me lad, and now it's up to us to rig up some sort of a dacint sate, and tag a woman along half the time. You thick-tongued descindint of a bagpipe baboon, what did you sind me in there for?"

"Maybe a little of it will tire her," groaned Dannie.

"It will if she undertakes to follow me," Jimmy said. "I know where horse-weeds grow giraffe high."

Then they went back to work, and presently many savory odors began to steal from the cabin. Whereat Jimmy looked at Dannie, and winked an 'I-told-you-so' wink. A garden grows fast under the hands of two strong men really working, and by the time the first slice of sugar-cured ham from the smoke house for that season struck the sizzling skillet, and Mary very meekly called from the back door to know if one of them wanted to dig a little horse radish, the garden was almost ready for planting. Then they went into the cabin and ate fragrant, thick slices of juicy fried ham, seasoned with horse radish; fried eggs, freckled with the ham fat in which they were cooked; fluffy mashed potatoes, with a little well of melted butter in the center of the mound overflowing the sides; raisin pie, soda biscuit, and their own maple syrup.

"Ohumahoh!" said Jimmy. "I don't know as I hanker for city life so much as I sometimes think I do. What do you suppose the adulterated stuff we read about in papers tastes like?"

"I've often wondered," answered Dannie. "Look at some of the hogs and cattle that we see shipped from here to city markets. The folks that sell them would starve before they'd eat a bit o' them, yet somebody eats them, and what do ye suppose maple syrup made from hickory bark and brown sugar tastes like?"

"And cold-storage eggs, and cotton-seed butter, and even horse radish half turnip," added Mary. "Bate up the cream a little before you put it in your coffee, or it will be in lumps. Whin the cattle are on clover it raises so thick."

Jimmy speared a piece of salt-rising bread crust soaked in ham gravy made with cream, and said: "I wish I could bring that Thrid Man home with me to one meal of the real thing nixt time he strikes town. I belave he would injoy it. May I, Mary?"

Mary's face flushed slightly. "Depends on whin he comes, she said. "Of course, if I am cleaning house, or busy with something I can't put off——"

"Sure!" cried Jimmy. "I'd ask you before I brought him, because I'd want him to have something spicial. Some of this ham, and horse radish, and maple syrup to begin with, and thin your fried spring chicken and your stewed squirrel is a drame, Mary. Nobody iver makes turtle soup half so rich as yours, and your green peas in cream, and asparagus on toast is a rivilation—don't you rimimber 'twas Father Michael that said it? I ought to be able to find mushrooms in a few weeks, and I can taste your rhubarb pie over from last year. Gee! But I wish he'd come in strawberrying! Berries from the vines, butter in the crust, crame you have to bate to make it smooth—talk about shortcake!"

"What's wrong wi' cherry cobbler?" asked Dannie.

"Or blackberry pie?"

"Or greens cooked wi' bacon?"

"Or chicken pie?"

"Or catfish, rolled in cornmeal and fried in ham fat?"

"Or guineas stewed in cream, with hard-boiled eggs in the gravy?"

"Oh, stop!" cried the delighted Mary. "It makes me dead tired thinkin' how I'll iver be cookin' all you'll want. Sure, have him come, and both of you can pick out the things you like the best, and I'll fix thim for him. Pure, fresh stuff might be a trate to a city man. When Dolan took sister Katie to New York with him, his boss sent them to a five-dollar-a-day house, and they thought they was some up. By the third day poor Katie was cryin' for a square male. She couldn't touch the butter, the eggs made her sick, and the cold-storage meat and chicken never got nearer her stomach than her nose. So she just ate fish, because they were fresh, and she ate, and she ate, till if you mintion New York to poor Katie she turns pale, and tastes fish. She vows and declares that she feeds her chickens and hogs better food twice a day than people fed her in New York."

"I'll bet my new milk pail the grub we eat ivery day would be a trate that would raise him," said Jimmy. "Provided his taste ain't so depraved with saltpeter and chalk he don't know fresh, pure food whin he tastes it. I understand some of the victims really don't."

"Your new milk pail?" questioned Mary.

"That's what!" said Jimmy." The next time I go to town I'm goin' to get you two."

"But I only need one," protested Mary. "Instead of two, get me a new dishpan. Mine leaks, and smears the stove and table."

"Be Gorry!" sighed Jimmy. "There goes me tongue, lettin' me in for it again. I'll look over the skins, and if any of thim are ripe, I'll get you a milk pail and a dishpan the nixt time I go to town. And, by gee! If that dandy big coon hide I got last fall looks good, I'm going to comb it up, and work the skin fine, and send it to the Thrid Man, with me complimints. I don't feel right about him yet. Wonder what his name railly is, and where he lives, or whether I killed him complate."

"Any dry goods man in town can tell ye," said Dannie.

"Ask the clerk in the hotel," suggested Mary.

"You've said it," cried Jimmy. "That's the stuff! And I can find out whin he will be here again."

Two hours more they faithfully worked on the garden, and then Jimmy began to grow restless.

"Ah, go on!" cried Mary. "You have done all that is needed just now, and more too. There won't any fish bite to-day, but you can have the pleasure of stringin' thim poor sufferin' worms on a hook and soaking thim in the river."

"'Sufferin' worms!' Sufferin' Job!" cried Jimmy. "What nixt? Go on, Dannie, get your pole!"

Dannie went. As he came back Jimmy was sprinkling a thin layer of earth over the bait in the can. "Why not come along, Mary?" he suggested.

"I'm not done planting my seeds," she answered. "I'll be tired when I am, and I thought that place wasn't fixed for me yet."

"We can't fix that till a little later," said Jimmy. "We can't tell where it's going to be grassy and shady yet, and the wood is too wet to fix a sate."

"Any kind of a sate will do," said Mary. "I guess you better not try to make one out of the Kingfisher stump. If you take it out it may change the pool and drive away the Bass."

"Sure!" cried Jimmy. "What a head you've got! We'll have to find some other stump for a sate."

"I don't want to go until it gets dry under foot, and warmer" said Mary. "You boys go on. I'll till you whin I am riddy to go."

"There!" said Jimmy, when well on the way to the river. "What did I tell you? Won't go if she has the chance! Jist wants to be ASKED."

"I dinna pretend to know women," said Dannie gravely. "But whatever Mary does is all richt with me."

"So I've obsarved," remarked Jimmy. "Now, how will we get at this fishin' to be parfectly fair?"

"Tell ye what I think," said Dannie. "I think we ought to pick out the twa best places about the Black Bass pool, and ye take ane fra yours and I'll take the ither fra mine, and then we'll each fish from his own place."

"Nothing fair about that," answered Jimmy. "You might just happen to strike the bed where he lays most, and be gettin' bites all the time, and me none; or I might strike it and you be left out. And thin there's days whin the wind has to do, and the light. We ought to change places ivery hour."

"There's nothing fair in that either," broke in Dannie. "I might have him tolled up to my place, and juist be feedin' him my bait, and here you'd come along and prove by your watch that my time was up, and take him when I had him all ready to bite."

"That's so for you!" hurried in Jimmy. "I'll be hanged if I'd leave a place by the watch whin I had a strike!"

"Me either," said Dannie. "'Tis past human nature to ask it. I'll tell ye what we'll do. We'll go to work and rig up a sort of a bridge where it's so narrow and shallow, juist above Kingfisher shoals, and then we'll toss up fra sides. Then each will keep to his side. With a decent pole either of us can throw across the pool, and both of us can fish as we please. Then each fellow can pick his bait, and cast or fish deep as he thinks best. What d'ye say to that?"

"I don't see how anything could be fairer than that," said Jimmy. "I don't want to fish for anything but the Bass. I'm goin' back and get our rubber boots, and you be rollin' logs, and we'll build that crossing right now."

"All richt," said Dannie.

So they laid aside their poles and tackle, and Dannie rolled logs and gathered material for the bridge, while Jimmy went back after their boots. Then both of them entered the water and began clearing away drift and laying the foundations. As the first log of the crossing lifted above the water Dannie paused.

"How about the Kingfisher?" he asked. "Winna this scare him away?"

"Not if he ain't a domn fool," said Jimmy; "and if he is, let him go!"

"Seems like the river would no be juist richt without him," said Dannie, breaking off a spice limb and nibbling the fragrant buds. "Let's only use what we bare need to get across. And where will we fix fra Mary?"

"Oh, git out!" said Jimmy. "I ain't goin' to fool with that."

"Well, we best fix a place. Then we can tell her we fixed it, and it's all ready."

"Sure!" cried Jimmy. "You are catchin' it from your neighbor. Till her a place is all fixed and watin', and you couldn't drag her here with a team of oxen. Till her you are GOING to fix it soon, and she'll come to see if you've done it, if she has to be carried on a stritcher."

So they selected a spot that they thought would be all right for Mary, and not close enough to disturb the Bass and the Kingfisher, rolled two logs, and fished a board that had been carried by a freshet from the water and laid it across them, and decided that would have to serve until they could do better.

Then they sat astride the board, Dannie drew out a coin, and they tossed it to see which was heads and tails. Dannie won heads. Then they tossed to see which bank was heads or tails, and the right, which was on Rainbow side, came heads. So Jimmy was to use the bridge. Then they went home, and began the night work. The first thing Jimmy espied was the barrel containing the milk pail. He fished out the pail, and while Dannie fed the stock, shoveled manure, and milked, Jimmy pounded out the dents, closed the bullet holes, emptied the bait into it, half filled it with mellow earth, and went to Mary for some corn meal to sprinkle on the top to feed the worms.

At four o'clock the next morning, Dannie was up feeding, milking, scraping plows, and setting bolts. After breakfast they piled their implements on a mudboat, which Dannie drove, while Jimmy rode one of his team, and led the other, and opened the gates. They began on Dannie's field, because it was closest, and for the next two weeks, unless it were too rainy to work, they plowed, harrowed, lined off, and planted the seed.

The blackbirds followed along the furrows picking up grubs, the crows cawed from high tree tops, the bluebirds twittered about hollow stumps and fence rails, the wood thrushes sang out their souls in the thickets across the river, and the King Cardinal of Rainbow Bottom whistled to split his throat from the giant sycamore. Tender greens were showing along the river and in the fields, and the purple of red-bud mingled with the white of wild plum all along the Wabash.

The sunny side of the hill that sloped down to Rainbow Bottom was a mass of spring beauties, anemones, and violets; thread-like ramps rose rank to the scent among them, and round ginger leaves were thrusting their folded heads through the mold. The Kingfisher was cleaning his house and fishing from his favorite stump in the river, while near him, at the fall of every luckless worm that missed its hold on a blossom-whitened thorn tree, came the splash of the great Black Bass. Every morning the Bass took a trip around Horseshoe Bend food hunting, and the small fry raced for life before his big, shear-like jaws. During the heat of noon he lay in the deep pool below the stump, and rested; but when evening came he set out in search of supper, and frequently he felt so good that he leaped clear of the water, and fell back with a splash that threw shining spray about him, or lashed out with his tail and sent widening circles of waves rolling from his lurking place. Then the Kingfisher rattled with all his might, and flew for the tunnel in the embankment.

Some of these days the air was still, the earth warmed in the golden sunshine, and murmured a low song of sleepy content. Some days the wind raised, whirling dead leaves before it, and covering the earth with drifts of plum, cherry, and apple bloom, like late falling snow. Then great black clouds came sweeping across the sky, and massed above Rainbow Bottom. The lightning flashed as if the heavens were being cracked open, and the rolling thunder sent terror to the hearts of man and beast. When the birds flew for shelter, Dannie and Jimmy unhitched their horses, and raced for the stables to escape the storm, and to be with Mary, whom electricity made nervous.

They would sit on the little front porch, and watch the greedy earth drink the downpour. They could almost see the grass and flowers grow. When the clouds scattered, the thunder grew fainter; and the sun shone again between light sprinkles of rain. Then a great, glittering rainbow set its arch in the sky, and it planted one of its feet in Horseshoe Bend, and the other so far away they could not even guess where.

If it rained lightly, in a little while Dannie and Jimmy could go back to their work afield. If the downpour was heavy, and made plowing impossible, they pulled weeds, and hoed in the garden. Dannie discoursed on the wholesome freshness of the earth, and Jimmy ever waited a chance to twist his words, and ring in a laugh on him. He usually found it. Sometimes, after a rain, they took their bait cans, and rods, and went down to the river to fish.

If one could not go, the other religiously refrained from casting bait into the pool where the Black Bass lay. Once, when they were fishing together, the Bass rose to a white moth, skittered over the surface by Dannie late in the evening, and twice Jimmy had strikes which he averred had taken the arm almost off him, but neither really had the Bass on his hook. They kept to their own land, and fished when they pleased, for game laws and wardens were unknown to them.

Truth to tell, neither of them really hoped to get the Bass before fall. The water was too high in the spring. Minnows were plentiful, and as Jimmy said, "It seemed as if the domn plum tree just rained caterpillars." So they bided their time, and the signs prohibiting trespass on all sides of their land were many and emphatic, and Mary had instructions to ring the dinner bell if she caught sight of any strangers.

The days grew longer, and the sun was insistent. Untold miles they trudged back and forth across their land, guiding their horses, jerked about with plows, their feet weighted with the damp, clinging earth, and their clothing pasted to their wet bodies. Jimmy was growing restless. Never in all his life had he worked so faithfully as that spring, and never had his visits to Casey's so told on him. No matter where they started, or how hard they worked, Dannie was across the middle of the field, and helping Jimmy before the finish. It was always Dannie who plowed on, while Jimmy rode to town for the missing bolt or buckle, and he generally rolled from his horse into a fence corner, and slept the remainder of the day on his return.

The work and heat were beginning to tire him, and his trips to Casey's had been much less frequent than he desired. He grew to feel that between them Dannie and Mary were driving him, and a desire to balk at slight cause, gathered in his breast. He deliberately tied his team in a fence corner, lay down, and fell asleep. The clanging of the supper bell aroused him. He opened his eyes, and as he rose, found that Dannie had been to the barn, and brought a horse blanket to cover him. Well as he knew anything, Jimmy knew that he had no business sleeping in fence corners so early in the season. With candor he would have admitted to himself that a part of his brittle temper came from aching bones and rheumatic twinges. Some way, the sight of Dannie swinging across the field, looking as fresh as in the early morning, and the fact that he had carried a blanket to cover him, and the further fact that he was wild for drink, and could think of no excuse on earth for going to town, brought him to a fighting crisis.

Dannie turned his horses at Jimmy's feet.

"Come on, Jimmy, supper bell has rung," he cried. "We mustn't keep Mary waiting. She wants us to help her plant the sweet potatoes to-nicht."

Jimmy rose, and his joints almost creaked. The pain angered him. He leaned forward and glared at Dannie.

"Is there one minute of the day whin you ain't thinkin' about my wife?" he demanded, oh, so slowly, and so ugly!

Dannie met his hateful gaze squarely. "Na a minute," he answered, "excepting when I am thinking about ye."

"The Hell you say!" exploded the astonished Jimmy.

Dannie stepped out of the furrow, and came closer. "See here, Jimmy Malone," he said. "Ye ain't forgot the nicht when I told ye I loved Mary, with all my heart, and that I'd never love another woman. I sent ye to tell her fra me, and to ask if I might come to her. And ye brought me her answer. It's na your fault that she preferred ye. Everybody did. But it IS your fault that I've stayed on here. I tried to go, and ye wouldna let me. So for fifteen years, ye have lain with the woman I love, and I have lain alone in a few rods of ye. If that ain't Man-Hell, try some other on me, and see if it will touch me! I sent ye to tell her that I loved her; have I ever sent ye to tell her that I've quit? I should think you'd know, by this time, that I'm na quitter. Love her! Why, I love her till I can see her standin' plain before me, when I know she's a mile away. Love her! Why, I can smell her any place I am, sweeter than any flower I ever held to my face. Love her! Till the day I dee I'll love her. But it ain't any fault of yours, and if ye've come to the place where I worry ye, that's the place where I go, as I wanted to on the same day ye brought Mary to Rainbow Bottom."

Jimmy's gray jaws fell open. Jimmy's sullen eyes cleared. He caught Dannie by the arm.

"For the love of Hivin, what did I say, Dannie?" he panted. "I must have been half asleep. Go! You go! You leave Rainbow Bottom! Thin, by God, I go too! I won't stay here without you, not a day. If I had to take my choice between you, I'd give up Mary before I'd give up the best frind I iver had. Go! I guess not, unless I go with you! She can go to———"

"Jimmy! Jimmy!" cautioned Dannie.

"I mane ivery domn word of it," said Jimmy. "I think more of you, than I iver did of any woman."

Dannie drew a deep breath. "Then why in the name of God did ye SAY that thing to me? I have na betrayed your trust in me, not ever, Jimmy, and ye know it. What's the matter with ye?"

Jimmy heaved a deep sigh, and rubbed his hands across his hot, angry face. "Oh, I'm just so domn sore!" he said. "Some days I get about wild. Things haven't come out like I thought they would."

"Jimmy, if ye are in trouble, why do ye na tell me? Canna I help ye? Have'nt I always helped ye if I could?"

"Yes, you have," said Jimmy. "Always, been a thousand times too good to me. But you can't help here. I'm up agin it alone, but put this in your pipe, and smoke it good and brown, if you go, I go. I don't stay here without you."

"Then it's up to ye na to make it impossible for me to stay," said Dannie.

"After this, I'll try to be carefu'. I've had no guard on my lips. I've said whatever came into my heid."

The supper bell clanged sharply a second time.

"That manes more Hivin on the Wabash," said Jimmy. "Wish I had a bracer before I face it."

"How long has it been, Jimmy?" asked Dannie.

"Etarnity!" replied Jimmy briefly.

Dannie stood thinking, and then light broke. Jimmy was always short of money in summer. When trapping was over, and before any crops were ready, he was usually out of funds. Dannie hesitated, and then he said, "Would a small loan be what ye need, Jimmy?"

Jimmy's eyes gleamed. "It would put new life into me," he cried. "Forgive me, Dannie. I am almost crazy."

Dannie handed over a coin, and after supper Jimmy went to town. Then Dannie saw his mistake. He had purchased peace for himself, but what about Mary?

Chapter VI

THE HEART OF MARY MALONE

"This is the job that was done with the reaper,
If we hustle we can do it ourselves,
Thus securing to us a little cheaper,
The bread and pie upon our pantry shelves.

Eat this wheat, by and by,
On this beautiful Wabash shore,
Drink this rye, by and by,
Eat and drink on this beautiful shore."

So sang Jimmy as he drove through the wheat, oats and rye accompanied by the clacking machinery. Dannie stopped stacking sheaves to mop his warm, perspiring face and to listen. Jimmy always with an eye to the effect he was producing immediately broke into wilder parody:

"Drive this mower, a little slower,
On this beautiful Wabash shore,
Cuttin' wheat to buy our meat,
Cuttin' oats, to buy our coats,
Also pants, if we get the chance.

By and by, we'll cut the rye,
But I bet my hat I drink that, I drink that.
Drive this mower a little slower,
In this wheat, in this wheat, by and by."

The larks scolded, fluttering over head, for at times the reaper overtook their belated broods. The bobolinks danced and chattered on stumps and fences, in an agony of suspense, when their nests were approached, and cried pitifully if they were destroyed. The chewinks flashed from the ground to the fences and trees, and back, crying "Che-wink?" "Che-wee!" to each other, in such excitement that they appeared to be in danger of flirting off their long tails. The quail ran about the shorn fields, and excitedly called from fence riders to draw their flocks into the security of Rainbow Bottom.

Frightened hares bounded through the wheat, and if the cruel blade sheared into their nests, Dannie gathered the wounded and helpless of the scattered broods in his hat, and carried them to Mary.

Then came threshing, which was a busy time, but after that, through the long hot days of late July and August, there was little to do afield, and fishing was impossible. Dannie grubbed fence corners, mended fences, chopped and corded wood for winter, and in spare time read his books. For the most part

Jimmy kept close to Dannie. Jimmy's temper never had been so variable. Dannie was greatly troubled, for despite Jimmy's protests of devotion, he flared at a word, and sometimes at no word at all. The only thing in which he really seemed interested was the coon skin he was dressing to send to Boston. Over that he worked by the hour, sometimes with earnest face, and sometimes he raised his head, and let out a whoop that almost frightened Mary. At such times he was sure to go on and give her some new detail of the hunt for the fifty coons, that he had forgotten to tell her before.

He had been to the hotel, and learned the Thread Man's name and address, and found that he did not come regularly, and no one knew when to expect him; so when he had combed and brushed the fur to its finest point, and worked the skin until it was velvet soft, and bleached it until it was muslin white, he made it into a neat package and sent it with his compliments to the Boston man. After he had waited for a week, he began going to town every day to the post office for the letter he expected, and coming home much worse for a visit to Casey's. Since plowing time he had asked Dannie for money as he wanted it, telling him to keep an account, and he would pay him in the fall. He seemed to forget or not to know how fast his bills grew.

Then came a week in August when the heat invaded even the cool retreat along the river. Out on the highway passing wheels rolled back the dust like water, and raised it in clouds after them. The rag weeds hung wilted heads along the road. The goldenrod and purple ironwort were dust-colored and dust-choked. The trees were thirsty, and their leaves shriveling. The river bed was bare its width in places, and while the Kingfisher made merry with his family, and rattled, feasting from Abram Johnson's to the Gar-hole, the Black Bass sought its deep pool, and lay still. It was a rare thing to hear it splash in those days.

The prickly heat burned until the souls of men were tried. Mary slipped listlessly about or lay much of the time on a couch beside a window, where a breath of air stirred. Despite the good beginning he had made in the spring, Jimmy slumped with the heat and exposures he had risked, and was hard to live with.

Dannie was not having a good time himself. Since Jimmy's wedding, life had been all grind to Dannie, but he kept his reason, accepted his lot, and ground his grist with patience and such cheer as few men could have summoned to the aid of so poor a cause. Had there been any one to notice it, Dannie was tired and heat-ridden also, but as always, Dannie sank self, and labored uncomplainingly with Jimmy's problems. On a burning August morning Dannie went to breakfast, and found Mary white and nervous, little prepared to eat, and no sign of Jimmy.

"Jimmy sleeping?" he asked.

"I don't know where Jimmy is," Mary answered coldly.

"Since when?" asked Dannie, gulping coffee, and taking hasty bites, for he had begun his breakfast supposing that Jimmy would come presently.

"He left as soon as you went home last night," she said, "and he has not come back yet."

Dannie did not know what to say. Loyal to the bone to Jimmy, loving each hair on the head of Mary Malone, and she worn and neglected; the problem was heartbreaking in any solution he attempted, and he felt none too well himself. He arose hastily, muttering something about getting the work done. He brought in wood and water, and asked if there was anything more he could do.

"Sure!" said Mary, in a calm, even voice. "Go to the barn, and shovel manure for Jimmy Malone, and do all the work he shirks, before you do anything for yoursilf."

Dannie always had admitted that he did not understand women, but he understood a plain danger signal, and he almost ran from the cabin. In the fear that Mary might think he had heeded her hasty words, he went to his own barn first, just to show her that he did not do Jimmy's work. The flies and mosquitoes were so bad he kept his horses stabled through the day, and turned them to pasture at night. So their stalls were to be cleaned, and he set to work. When he had finished his own barn, as he had nothing else to do, he went on to Jimmy's. He had finished the stalls, and was sweeping when he heard a sound at the back door, and turning saw Jimmy clinging to the casing, unable to stand longer. Dannie sprang to him, and helped him inside. Jimmy sank to the floor. Dannie caught up several empty grain sacks, folded them, and pushed them under Jimmy's head for a pillow.

"Dannish, didsh shay y'r nash'nal flowerish wash shisle?" asked Jimmy.

"Yes," said Dannie, lifting the heavy auburn head to smooth the folds from the sacks.

"Whysh like me?"

"I dinna," answered Dannie wearily.

"Awful jagsh on," murmured Jimmy, sighed heavily, and was off. His clothing was torn and dust-covered, his face was purple and bloated, and his hair was dusty and disordered. He was a repulsive sight. As Dannie straightened Jimmy's limbs he thought he heard a step. He lifted his head and leaned forward to listen.

"Dannie Micnoun?" called the same even, cold voice he had heard at breakfast. "Have you left me, too?"

Dannie sprang for a manger. He caught a great armload of hay, and threw it over Jimmy. He gave one hurried toss to scatter it, for Mary was in the barn. As he turned to interpose his body between her and the manger, which partially screened Jimmy, his heart sickened. He was too late. She had seen. Frightened to the soul, he stared at her. She came a step closer, and with her foot gave a hand of Jimmy's that lay exposed a contemptuous shove.

"You didn't get him complately covered," she said. "How long have you had him here?"

Dannie was frightened into speech. "Na a minute, Mary; he juist came in when I heard ye. I was trying to spare ye."

"Him, you mane," she said, in that same strange voice. "I suppose you give him money, and he has a bottle, and he's been here all night."

"Mary," said Dannie, "that's na true. I have furnished him money. He'd mortgage the farm, or do something worse if I didna; but I dinna WHERE he has been all nicht, and in trying to cover him, my only thought was to save ye pain."

"And whin you let him spind money you know you'll never get back, and loaf while you do his work, and when you lie mountain high, times without number, who is it for?"

Then fifteen years' restraint slid from Dannie like a cloak, and in the torture of his soul his slow tongue outran all its previous history.

"Ye!" he shouted. "It's fra Jimmy, too, but ye first. Always ye first!" Mary began to tremble. Her white cheeks burned red. Her figure straightened, and her hands clenched.

"On the cross! Will you swear it?" she cried.

"On the sacred body of Jesus Himself, if I could face Him," answered Dannie. "anything! Everything is fra ye first, Mary!"

"Then why?" she panted between gasps for breath. "Tell me why? If you have cared for me enough to stay here all these years and see that I had the bist tratemint you could get for me, why didn't you care for me enough more to save me this? Oh, Dannie, tell me why?"

And then she shook with strangled sobs until she scarce could stand alone. Dannie Macnoun cleared the space between them and took her in his arms. Her trembling hands clung to him, her head dropped on his breast, and the perfume of her hair in his nostrils drove him mad. Then the tense bulk of her body struck against him, and horror filled his soul. One second he held her, the next, Jimmy smothering under the hay, threw up an arm, and called like a petulant child, "Dannie! Make shun quit shinish my fashe!"

And Dannie awoke to the realization that Mary was another man's, and that man, one who trusted him completely. The problem was so much too big for poor Dannie that reason kindly slipped a cog. He broke from the grasp of the woman, fled through the back door, and took to the woods.

He ran as if fiends were after him, and he ran and ran. And when he could run no longer, he walked, but he went on. Just on and on. He crossed forests and fields, orchards and highways, streams and rivers, deep woods and swamps, and on, and on he went. He felt nothing, and saw nothing, and thought nothing, save to go on, always on. In the dark he stumbled on and through the day he staggered on, and he stopped for nothing, save at times to lift water to his parched lips.

The bushes took his hat, the thorns ripped his shirt, the water soaked his shoes and they spread and his feet came through and the stones cut them until they bled. Leaves and twigs stuck in his hair, and his eyes grew bloodshot, his lips and tongue swollen, and when he could go no further on his feet, he crawled on his knees, until at last he pitched forward on his face and lay still. The tumult was over and Mother Nature set to work to see about repairing damages.

Dannie was so badly damaged, soul, heart, and body, that she never would have been equal to the task, but another woman happened that way and she helped. Dannie was carried to a house and a doctor dressed his hurts. When the physician got down to first principles, and found a big, white-bodied, fine-faced Scotchman in the heart of the wreck, he was amazed. A wild man, but not a whiskey bloat. A crazy man, but not a maniac. He stood long beside Dannie as he lay unconscious.

"I'll take oath that man has wronged no one," he said. "What in the name of God has some woman been doing to him?"

He took money from Dannie's wallet and bought clothing to replace the rags he had burned. He filled Dannie with nourishment, and told the woman who found him that when he awoke, if he did not remember, to tell him that his name was Dannie Macnoun, and that he lived in Rainbow Bottom, Adams County. Because just at that time Dannie was halfway across the state.

A day later he awoke, in a strange room and among strange faces. He took up life exactly where he left off. And in his ears, as he remembered his flight, rang the awful cry uttered by Mary Malone, and not until then did there come to Dannie the realization that she had been driven to seek him for help, because her woman's hour was upon her. Cold fear froze Dannie's soul.

He went back by railway and walked the train most of the way. He dropped from the cars at the water tank and struck across country, and again he ran. But this time it was no headlong flight. Straight as a homing bird went Dannie with all speed, toward the foot of the Rainbow and Mary Malone.

The Kingfisher sped rattling down the river when Dannie came crashing along the bank.

"Oh, God, let her be alive!" prayed Dannie as he leaned panting against a tree for an instant, because he was very close now and sickeningly afraid. Then he ran on. In a minute it would be over. At the next turn he could see the cabins. As he dashed along, Jimmy Malone rose from a log and faced him. A white Jimmy, with black- ringed eyes and shaking hands.

"Where the Hell have you been?" Jimmy demanded.

"Is she dead?" cried Dannie.

"The doctor is talking scare," said Jimmy. "But I don't scare so easy. She's never been sick in her life, and she has lived through it twice before, why should she die now? Of course the kid is dead again," he added angrily.

Dannie shut his eyes and stood still. He had helped plant star- flowers on two tiny cross-marked mounds at Five Mile Hill. Now, there were three. Jimmy had worn out her love for him, that was plain. "Why should she die now?" To Dannie it seemed that question should have been, "Why should she live?"

Jimmy eyed him belligerently. "Why in the name of sinse did you cut out whin I was off me pins?" he growled. "Of course I don't blame you for cutting that kind of a party, me for the woods, all right, but what I can't see is why you couldn't have gone for the doctor and waited until I'd slept it off before you wint."

"I dinna know she was sick," answered Dannie. "I deserve anything ony ane can say to me, and it's all my fault if she dees, but this ane thing ye got to say ye know richt noo, Jimmy. Ye got to say ye know that I dinna understand Mary was sick when I went."

"Sure! I've said that all the time," agreed Jimmy. "But what I don't understand is, WHY you went! I guess she thinks it was her fault. I came out here to try to study it out. The nurse-woman, domn pretty girl, says if you don't get back before midnight, it's all up. You're just on time, Dannie. The talk in the house is that she'll wink out if you don't prove to her that she didn't drive you away. She is about crazy over it. What did she do to you?"

"Nothing!" exclaimed Dannie. "She was so deathly sick she dinna what she was doing. I can see it noo, but I dinna understand then."

"That's all right," said Jimmy. "She didn't! She kapes moaning over and over 'What did I do?' You hustle in and fix it up with her. I'm getting tired of all this racket."

All Dannie heard was that he was to go to Mary. He went up the lane, across the garden, and stepped in at the back door. Beside the table stood a comely young woman, dressed in blue and white stripes. She was doing something with eggs and milk. She glanced at Dannie, and finished filling a glass. As she held it to the light, "Is your name Macnoun?" she inquired.

"Yes," said Dannie.

"Dannie Macnoun?" she asked.

"Yes," said Dannie.

"Then you are the medicine needed here just now," she said, as if that were the most natural statement in the world. "Mrs. Malone seems to have an idea that she offended you, and drove you from home, just prior to her illness, and as she has been very sick, she is in no condition to bear other trouble. You understand?"

"Do ye understand that I couldna have gone if I had known she was ill?" asked Dannie in turn.

"From what she has said in delirium I have been sure of that," replied the nurse. "It seems you have been the stay of the family for years. I have a very high opinion of you, Mr. Macnoun. Wait until I speak to her."

The nurse vanished, presently returned, and as Dannie passed through the door, she closed it after him, and he stood still, trying to see in the dim light. That great snowy stretch, that must be the bed. That tumbled dark circle, that must be Mary's hair. That dead white thing beneath it, that must be Mary's face. Those burning lights, flaming on him, those must be Mary's eyes. Dannie stepped softly across the room, and bent over the bed. He tried hard to speak naturally.

"Mary" he said, "oh, Mary, I dinna know ye were ill! Oh, believe me, I dinna realize ye were suffering pain."

She smiled faintly, and her lips moved. Dannie bent lower.

"Promise," she panted. "Promise you will stay now."

Her hand fumbled at her breast, and then she slipped on the white cover a little black cross. Dannie knew what she meant. He laid his hand on the emblem precious to her, and said softly, "I swear I never will leave ye again, Mary Malone."

A great light swept into her face, and she smiled happily.

"Now ye," said Dannie. He slipped the cross into her hand. "Repeat after me," he said. "I promise I will get well, Dannie."

"I promise I will get well, Dannie, if I can," said Mary.

"Na," said Dannie. "That winna do. Repeat what I said, and remember it is on the cross. Life hasna been richt for ye, Mary, but if ye will get well, before the Lord in some way we will make it happier. Ye will get well?"

"I promise I will get well, Dannie," said Mary Malone, and Dannie softly left the room.

Outside he said to the nurse, "What can I do?"

She told him everything of which she could think that would be of benefit.

"Now tell me all ye know of what happened," commanded Dannie.

"After you left," said the nurse, "she was in labor, and she could not waken her husband, and she grew frightened and screamed. There were men passing out on the road. They heard her, and came to see what was the matter."

"Strangers?" shuddered Dannie, with dry lips.

"No, neighbors. One man went for the nearest woman, and the other drove to town for a doctor. They had help here almost as soon as you could. But, of course, the shock was a very dreadful thing, and the heat of the past few weeks has been enervating."

"Ane thing more," questioned Dannie. "Why do her children dee?"

"I don't know about the others," answered the nurse. "This one simply couldn't be made to breathe. It was a strange thing. It was a fine big baby, a boy, and it seemed perfect, but we couldn't save it. I never worked harder. They told me she had lost two others, and we tried everything of which we could think. It just seemed as if it had grown a lump of flesh, with no vital spark in it."

Dannie turned, went out of the door, and back along the lane to the river where he had left Jimmy. "'A lump of flesh with na vital spark in it,'" he kept repeating. "I dinna but that is the secret. She is almost numb with misery. All these days when she's been without hope, and these awful nichts, when she's watched and feared alone, she has no wished to perpetuate him in children who might be like him, and so at their coming the 'vital spark' is na in them. Oh, Jimmy, Jimmy, have ye Mary's happiness and those three little graves to answer for?"

He found Jimmy asleep where he had left him. Dannie shook him awake. "I want to talk with ye," he said.

Jimmy sat up, and looked into Dannie's face. He had a complaint on his lips but it died there. He tried to apologize. "I am almost dead for sleep," he said. "There has been no rest for anyone here. What do you think?"

"I think she will live," said Dannie dryly. "In spite of your neglect, and my cowardice, I think she will live to suffer more frae us."

Jimmy's mouth opened, but for once no sound issued. The drops of perspiration raised on his forehead.

Dannie sat down, and staring at him Jimmy saw that there were patches of white hair at his temples that had been brown a week before; his colorless face was sunken almost to the bone, and there was a peculiar twist about his mouth. Jimmy's heart weighed heavily, his tongue stood still, and he was afraid to the marrow in his bones.

"I think she will live," repeated Dannie. "And about the suffering more, we will face that like men, and see what can be done about it. This makes three little graves on the hill, Jimmy, what do they mean to ye?"

"Domn bad luck," said Jimmy promptly.

"Nothing more?" asked Dannie. "Na responsibility at all. Ye are the father of those children. Have ye never been to the doctor, and asked why ye lost them?"

"No, I haven't," said Jimmy.

"That is ane thing we will do now," said Dannie, "and then we will do more, much more."

"What are you driving at?" asked Jimmy.

"The secret of Mary's heart," said Dannie.

The cold sweat ran from the pores of Jimmy's body. He licked his dry lips, and pulled his hat over his eyes, that he might watch Dannie from under the brim.

"We are twa big, strong men," said Dannie. "For fifteen years we have lived here wi' Mary. The night ye married her, the licht of happiness went out for me. But I shut my mouth, and shouldered my burden, and went on with my best foot first; because if she had na refused me, I should have married her, and then ye would have been the one to suffer. If she had chosen me, I should have married her, juist as ye did. Oh, I've never forgotten that! So I have na been a happy mon, Jimmy. We winna go into that any further, we've been over it once. It seems to be a form of torture especially designed fra me, though at times I must confess, it seems rough, and I canna see why, but we'll cut that off with this: life has been Hell's hottest sweat-box fra me these fifteen years."

Jimmy groaned aloud. Dannie's keen gray eyes seemed boring into the soul of the man before him, as he went on.

"Now how about ye? Ye got the girl ye wanted. Ye own a guid farm that would make ye a living, and save ye money every year. Ye have done juist what ye pleased, and as far as I could, I have helped ye. I've had my eye on ye pretty close, Jimmy, and if YE are a happy mon, I dinna but I'm content as I am. What's your trouble? Did ye find ye dinna love Mary after ye won her? Did ye murder your mither or blacken your soul with some deadly sin? Mon! If I had in my life what ye every day neglect and torture, Heaven would come doon, and locate at the foot of the Rainbow fra me. But, ye are no happy, Jimmy. Let's get at the root of the matter. While ye are unhappy, Mary will be also. We are responsible to God for her, and between us, she is empty armed, near to death, and almost dumb with misery. I have juist sworn to her on the cross she loves that if she will make ane more effort, and get well, we will make her happy. Now, how are we going to do it?"

Another great groan burst from Jimmy, and he shivered as if with a chill.

"Let us look ourselves in the face," Dannie went on, "and see what we lack.

What can we do fra her? What will bring a song to her lips, licht to her beautiful eyes, love to her heart, and a living child to her arms? Wake up, mon! By God, if ye dinna set to work with me and solve this problem, I'll shake a solution out of ye! What I must suffer is my own, but what's the matter with ye, and why, when she loved and married ye, are ye breakin' Mary's heart? Answer me, mon!"

Dannie reached over and snatched the hat from Jimmy's forehead, and stared at an inert heap. Jimmy lay senseless, and he looked like death. Dannie rushed down to the water with the hat, and splashed drops into Jimmy's face until he gasped for breath. When he recovered a little, he shrank from Dannie, and began to sob, as if he were a sick ten-year-old child.

"I knew you'd go back on me, Dannie," he wavered. "I've lost the only frind I've got, and I wish I was dead."

"I havena gone back on ye," persisted Dannie, bathing Jimmy's face. "Life means nothing to me, save as I can use it fra Mary, and fra ye. Be quiet, and sit up here, and help me work this thing out. Why are ye a discontented mon, always wishing fra any place save home? Why do ye spend all ye earn foolishly, so that ye are always hard up, when ye might have affluence? Why does Mary lose her children, and why does she noo wish she had na married ye?"

"Who said she wished she hadn't married me?" cried Jimmy.

"Do ye mean to say ye think she doesn't?" blazed Dannie.

"I ain't said anything!" exclaimed Jimmy.

"Na, and I seem to have damn poor luck gettin' ye TO say anything. I dinna ask fra tears, nor faintin' like a woman. Be a mon, and let me into the secret of this muddle. There is a secret, and ye know it. What is it? Why are ye breaking the heart o' Mary Malone? Answer me, or 'fore God I'll wring the answer fra your body!"

And Jimmy keeled over again. This time he was gone so far that Dannie was frightened into a panic, and called the doctor coming up the lane to Jimmy before he had time to see Mary. The doctor soon brought Jimmy around, prescribed quiet and sleep; talked about heart trouble developing, and symptoms of tremens, and Dannie poured on water, and gritted his teeth. And it ended by Jimmy being helped to Dannie's cabin, undressed, and put into bed, and then Dannie went over to see what he could do for the nurse. She looked at him searchingly.

"Mr. Macnoun, when were you last asleep?" she asked.

"I forget," answered Dannie.

"When did you last have a good hot meal?"

"I dinna know," replied Dannie.

"Drink that," said the nurse, handing him the bowl of broth she carried, and going back to the stove for another. "When I have finished making Mrs. Malone comfortable, I'm going to get you something to eat, and you are going to eat it. Then you are going to lie down on that cot where I can call you if I need you, and sleep six hours, and then you're going to wake up and watch by this door while I sleep my six. Even nurses must have some rest, you know."

"Ye first," said Dannie. "I'll be all richt when I get food. Since ye mention it,

I believe I am almost mad with hunger."

The nurse handed him another bowl of broth. "Just drink that, and drink slowly," she said, as she left the room.

Dannie could hear her speaking softly to Mary, and then all was quiet, and the girl came out and closed the door. She deftly prepared food for Dannie, and he ate all she would allow him, and begged for more; but she firmly told him her hands were full now, and she had no one to depend on but him to watch after the turn of the night. So Dannie lay down on the cot. He had barely touched it when he thought of Jimmy, so he got up quietly and started home. He had almost reached his back door when it opened, and Jimmy came out. Dannie paused, amazed at Jimmy's wild face and staring eyes.

"Don't you begin your cursed gibberish again," cried Jimmy, at sight of him. "I'm burning in all the tortures of fire now, and I'll have a drink if I smash down Casey's and steal it."

Dannie jumped for him, and Jimmy evaded him and fled. Dannie started after. He had reached the barn before he began to think. "I depend on you," the nurse had said. "Jimmy, wait!" he called. "Jimmy, have ye any money?" Jimmy was running along the path toward town. Dannie stopped. He stood staring after Jimmy for a second, and then he deliberately turned, went back, and lay down on the cot, where the nurse expected to find him when she wanted him to watch by the door of Mary Malone.

Chapter VII

THE APPLE OF DISCORD BECOMES A JOINTED ROD

"WHAT do you think about fishing, Dannie?" asked Jimmy Malone.

"There was a licht frost last nicht," said Dannie. "It begins to look that way. I should think a week more, especially if there should come a guid rain."

Jimmy looked disappointed. His last trip to town had ended in a sodden week in the barn, and at Dannie's cabin. For the first time he had carried whiskey home with him. He had insisted on Dannie drinking with him, and wanted to fight when he would not. He addressed the bottle, and Dannie, as the Sovereign Alchemist by turns, and "transmuted the leaden metal of life into pure gold" of a glorious drunk, until his craving was satisfied. Then he came back to work and reason one morning, and by the time Mary was about enough to notice him, he was Jimmy at his level best, and doing more than he had in years to try to interest and please her.

Mary had fully recovered, and appeared as strong as she ever had been, but there was a noticeable change in her. She talked and laughed with a gayety that seemed forced, and in the midst of it her tongue turned bitter, and Jimmy and Dannie fled before it.

The gray hairs multiplied on Dannie's head with rapidity. He had gone to the doctor, and to Mary's sister, and learned nothing more than the nurse could tell him. Dannie was willing to undertake anything in the world for Mary, but just how to furnish the "vital spark," to an unborn babe, was too big a problem for him. And Jimmy Malone was growing to be another. Heretofore, Dannie had borne the brunt of the work, and all of the worry. He had let Jimmy feel that his was the guiding hand. Jimmy's plans were followed whenever it was possible, and when it was not, Dannie started Jimmy's way, and gradually worked around to his own. But, there never had been a time between them, when things really came to a crisis, and Dannie took the lead, and said matters must go a certain way, that Jimmy had not acceded. In reality, Dannie always had been master.

Now he was not. Where he lost control he did not know. He had tried several times to return to the subject of how to bring back happiness to Mary, and Jimmy immediately developed symptoms of another attack of heart disease, a tendency to start for town, or openly defied him by walking away. Yet, Jimmy stuck to him closer than he ever had, and absolutely refused to go anywhere, or to do the smallest piece of work alone. Sometimes he grew sullen and morose when he was not drinking, and that was very unlike the gay Jimmy. Sometimes he grew wildly hilarious, as if he were bound to make such a racket that he could hear no sound save his own voice. So long as he stayed at home, helped with the work, and made an effort to please Mary, Dannie hoped for the best, but his hopes never grew so bright that they shut out an awful fear that was beginning to loom in the future. But he tried in every way to encourage Jimmy, and help him in the struggle he did not understand, so when he saw that Jimmy was disappointed about the fishing, he suggested that he should go alone.

"I guess not!" said Jimmy. "I'd rather go to confission than to go alone. What's the fun of fishin' alone? All the fun there is to fishin' is to watch the other fellow's eyes when you pull in a big one, and try to hide yours from him when he gets it. I guess not! What have we got to do?"

"Finish cutting the corn, and get in the pumpkins before there comes frost enough to hurt them."

"Well, come along!" said Jimmy. "Let's get it over. I'm going to begin fishing for that Bass the morning after the first black frost, if I do go alone. I mean it!"

"But ye said—" began Dannie.

"Hagginy!" cried Jimmy. "What a lot of time you've wasted if you've been kaping account of all the things I've said. Haven't you learned by this time that I lie twice to the truth once?"

Dannie laughed. "Dinna say such things, Jimmy. I hate to hear ye. Of course, I know about the fifty coons of the Canoper, and things like that; honest, I dinna believe ye can help it. But na man need lie about a serious matter, and when he knows he is deceiving another who trusts him." Jimmy became so white that he felt the color receding, and turned to hide his face. "Of course, about those fifty coons noo, what was the harm in that? Nobody believed it. That wasna deceiving any ane."

"Yes, but it was," answered Jimmy. "The Boston man belaved it, and I guiss he hasn't forgiven me, if he did take my hand, and drink with me. You know I haven't had a word from him about that coon skin. I worked awful hard on that skin. Some way, I tried to make it say to him again that I was sorry for that night's work. Sometimes I am afraid I killed the fellow."

"O-ho!" scoffed Dannie. "Men ain't so easy killed. I been thinkin' about it, too, and I'll tell ye what I think. I think he goes on long trips, and only gets home every four or five months. The package would have to wait. His folks wouldna try to send it after him. He was a monly fellow, all richt, and ye will hear fra him yet."

"I'd like to," said Jimmy, absently, beating across his palm a spray of goldenrod he had broken. "Just a line to tell me that he don't bear malice."

"Ye will get it," said Dannie. "Have a little patience. But that's your greatest fault, Jimmy. Ye never did have ony patience."

"For God's sake, don't begin on me faults again," snapped Jimmy. "I reckon I know me faults about as well as the nixt fellow. I'm so domn full of faults that I've thought a lot lately about fillin' up, and takin' a sleep on the railroad."

A new fear wrung Dannie's soul. "Ye never would, Jimmy," he implored.

"Sure not!" cried Jimmy. "I'm no good Catholic livin', but if it come to dyin', bedad I niver could face it without first confissin' to the praste, and that would give the game away. Let's cut out dyin', and cut corn!"

"That's richt," agreed Dannie. "And let's work like men, and then fish fra a week or so, before ice and trapping time comes again. I'll wager I can beat ye the first row."

"Bate!" scoffed Jimmy. "Bate! With them club-footed fingers of yours? You couldn't bate an egg. Just watch me! If you are enough of a watch to keep your hands runnin' at the same time."

Jimmy worked feverishly for an hour, and then he straightened and looked about him. On the left lay the river, its shores bordered with trees and bushes. Behind them was deep wood. Before them lay their open fields, sloping down to the bottom, the cabins on one side, and the kingfisher embankment on the other. There was a smoky haze in the air. As always the blackbirds clamored along the river. Some crows followed the workers at a distance, hunting for grains of corn, and over in the woods, a chewink scratched and rustled among the deep leaves as it searched for grubs. From time to time a flock of quail arose before them with a whirr and scattered down the fields, reassembling later at the call of their leader, from a rider of the snake fence, which inclosed the field.

"Bob, Bob White," whistled Dannie.

"Bob, Bob White," answered the quail.

"I got my eye on that fellow," said Jimmy. "When he gets a little larger, I'm going after him."

"Seems an awful pity to kill him," said Dannie. "People rave over the lark, but I vow I'd miss the quail most if they were both gone. They are getting scarce."

"Well, I didn't say I was going to kill the whole flock," said Jimmy. "I was just going to kill a few for Mary, and if I don't, somebody else will."

"Mary dinna need onything better than ane of her own fried chickens," said Dannie. "And its no true about hunters. We've the river on ane side, and the bluff on the other. If we keep up our fishing signs, and add hunting to them, and juist shut the other fellows out, the birds will come here like everything wild gathers in National Park, out West. Ye bet things know where they are taken care of, well enough."

Jimmy snipped a spray of purple ironwort with his corn-cutter, and stuck it through his suspender buckle. "I think that would be more fun than killin' them. If you're a dacint shot, and your gun is clane" (Jimmy remembered the crow that had escaped with the eggs at soap-making), "you pretty well know you're goin' to bring down anything you aim at. But it would be a dandy joke to shell a little corn as we husk it, and toll all the quail into Rainbow Bottom, and then kape the other fellows out. Bedad! Let's do it."

Jimmy addressed the quail:

"Quailie, quailie on the fince,
We think your singin's just imminse.
Stay right here, and live with us,
And the fellow that shoots you will strike a fuss."

"We can protect them all richt enough," laughed Dannie. "And when the snow comes we can feed Cardinals like cheekens. Wish when we threshed, we'd saved a few sheaves of wheat. They do that in Germany, ye know. The last sheaf of the harvest they put up on a long pole at Christmas, as a thank-offering to the birds fra their care of the crops. My father often told of it."

"That would be great," said Jimmy. "Now look how domn slow you are! Why didn't you mintion it at harvest? I'd like things comin' for me to take care of them. Gee! Makes me feel important just to think about it. Next year we'll do it, sure. They'd be a lot of company. A man could work in this field to-day, with all the flowers around him, and the colors of the leaves like a garden, and a lot of birds talkin' to him, and not feel afraid of being alone."

"Afraid?" quoted Dannie, in amazement.

For an instant Jimmy looked startled. Then his love of proving his point arose. "Yes, afraid!" he repeated stubbornly. "Afraid of being away from the sound of a human voice, because whin you are, the voices of the black divils of conscience come twistin' up from the ground in a little wiry whisper, and moanin' among the trees, and whistlin' in the wind, and rollin' in the thunder, and above all in the dark they screech, and shout, and roar, 'We're after you, Jimmy Malone! We've almost got you, Jimmy Malone! You're going to burn in Hell, Jimmy Malone!'"

Jimmy leaned toward Dannie, and began in a low voice, but he grew so excited as he tried to picture the thing that he ended in a scream, and even then Dannie's horrified eyes failed to recall him. Jimmy straightened, stared wildly behind him, and over the open, hazy field, where flowers bloomed, and birds called, and the long rows of shocks stood unconscious auditors of the strange scene. He lifted his hat, and wiped the perspiration from his dripping face with the sleeve of his shirt, and as he raised his arm, the corn- cutter flashed in the light.

"My God, it's awful, Dannie! It's so awful, I can't begin to tell you!"

Dannie's face was ashen. "Jimmy, dear auld fellow," he said, "how long has this been going on?"

"A million years," said Jimmy, shifting the corn-cutter to the hand that held his hat, that he might moisten his fingers with saliva and rub it across his parched lips.

"Jimmy, dear," Dannie's hand was on Jimmy's sleeve. "Have ye been to town in the nicht, or anything like that lately?"

"No, Dannie, dear, I ain't," sneered Jimmy, setting his hat on the back of his head and testing the corn-cutter with his thumb. "This ain't Casey's, me lad. I've no more call there, at this minute, than you have."

"It is Casey's, juist the same," said Dannie bitterly. "Dinna ye know the end of this sort of thing?"

"No, bedad, I don't!" said Jimmy. "If I knew any way to ind it, you can bet I've had enough. I'd ind it quick enough, if I knew how. But the railroad wouldn't be the ind. That would just be the beginnin'. Keep close to me, Dannie, and talk, for mercy sake, talk! Do you think we could finish the corn by noon?"

"Let's try!" said Dannie, as he squared his shoulders to adjust them to his new load. "Then we'll get in the pumpkins this afternoon, and bury the potatoes, and the cabbage and turnips, and then we're aboot fixed fra winter."

"We must take one day, and gather our nuts," suggested Jimmy, struggling to make his voice sound natural, "and you forgot the apples. We must bury thim too."

"That's so," said Dannie, "and when that's over, we'll hae nothing left to do but catch the Bass, and say farewell to the Kingfisher."

"I've already told you that I would relave you of all responsibility about the Bass," said Jimmy, "and when I do, you won't need trouble to make your adieus to the Kingfisher of the Wabash. He'll be one bird that won't be migrating this winter."

Dannie tried to laugh. "I'd like fall as much as any season of the year," he said, "if it wasna for winter coming next."

"I thought you liked winter, and the trampin' in the white woods, and trappin', and the long evenings with a book."

"I do," said Dannie. "I must have been thinkin' of Mary. She hated last winter so. Of course, I had to go home when ye were away, and the nichts were so long, and so cold, and mony of them alone. I wonder if we canna arrange fra one of her sister's girls to stay with her this winter?"

"What's the matter with me?" asked Jimmy.

"Nothing, if only ye'd stay," answered Dannie.

"All I'll be out of nights, you could put in one eye," said Jimmy. "I went last winter, and before, because whin they clamored too loud, I could be drivin' out the divils that way, for a while, and you always came for me, but even that won't be stopping it now. I wouldn't stick my head out alone after dark, not if I was dying!"

"Jimmy, ye never felt that way before," said Dannie. "Tell me what happened this summer to start ye."

"I've done a domn sight of faleing that you didn't know anything about," answered Jimmy. "I could work it off at Casey's for a while, but this summer things sort of came to a head, and I saw meself for fair, and before God, Dannie, I didn't like me looks."

"Well, then, I like your looks," said Dannie. "Ye are the best company I ever was in. Ye are the only mon I ever knew that I cared fra, and I care fra ye so much, I havna the way to tell ye how much. You're possessed with a damn fool idea, Jimmy, and ye got to shake it off. Such a great-hearted, big mon as ye! I winna have it! There's the dinner bell, and richt glad I am of it!"

That afternoon when pumpkin gathering was over and Jimmy had invited Mary out to separate the "punk" from the pumpkins, there was a wagon-load of good ones above what they would need for their use. Dannie proposed to take them to town and sell them. To his amazement Jimmy refused to go along.

"I told you this morning that Casey wasn't calling me at prisent," he said, "and whin I am not called I'd best not answer. I have promised Mary to top the onions and bury the cilery, and murder the bates."

"Do what wi' the beets?" inquired the puzzled Dannie.

"Kill thim! Kill thim stone dead. I'm too tinder-hearted to be burying anything but a dead bate, Dannie. That's a thousand years old, but laugh, like I knew you would, old Ramphirinkus! No, thank you, I don't go to town!"

Then Dannie was scared. "He's going to be dreadfully seek or go mad," he said.

So he drove to the village, sold the pumpkins, filled Mary's order for groceries, and then went to the doctor, and told him of Jimmy's latest developments.

"It is the drink," said that worthy disciple of Esculapius. "It's the drink! In time it makes a fool sodden and a bright man mad. Few men have sufficient brains to go crazy. Jimmy has. He must stop the drink."

On the street, Dannie encountered Father Michael. The priest stopped him to shake hands.

"How's Mary Malone?" he asked.

"She is quite well noo," answered Dannie, "but she is na happy. I live so close, and see so much, I know. I've thought of ye lately. I have thought of coming to see ye. I'm na of your religion, but Mary is, and what suits her is guid enough for me. I've tried to think of everything under the sun that might help, and among other things I've thought of ye. Jimmy was confirmed in your church, and he was more or less regular up to his marriage."

"Less, Mr. Macnoun, much less!" said the priest. "Since, not at all. Why do you ask?"

"He is sick," said Dannie. "He drinks a guid deal. He has been reckless about sleeping on the ground, and noo, if ye will make this confidential?"—the priest nodded—"he is talking aboot sleeping on the railroad, and he's having delusions. There are devils after him. He is the finest fellow ye ever knew, Father Michael. We've been friends all our lives. Ye have had much experience with men, and it ought to count fra something. From all ye know, and what I've told ye, could his trouble be cured as the doctor suggests?"

The priest did a queer thing. "You know him as no living man, Dannie," he said. "What do you think?"

Dannie's big hands slowly opened and closed. Then he fell to polishing the nails of one hand on the palm of the other. At last he answered, "If ye'd asked me that this time last year, I'd have said 'it's the drink,' at a jump. But times this summer, this morning, for instance, when he hadna a drop in three weeks, and dinna want ane, when he could have come wi' me to town, and wouldna, and there were devils calling him from the ground, and the trees, and the sky, out in the open cornfield, it looked bad."

The priest's eyes were boring into Dannie's sick face. "How did it look?" he asked briefly.

"It looked," said Dannie, and his voice dropped to a whisper, "it looked like he might carry a damned ugly secret, that it would be better fra him if ye, at least, knew."

"And the nature of that secret?"

Dannie shook his head. "Couldna give a guess at it! Known him all his life. My only friend. Always been togither. Square a mon as God ever made. There's na fault in him, if he'd let drink alone. Got more faith in him than any ane I ever knew. I wouldna trust mon on God's footstool, if I had to lose faith in Jimmy. Come to think of it, that 'secret' business is all old woman's scare. The drink is telling on him. If only he could be cured of that awful weakness, all heaven would come down and settle in Rainbow Bottom."

They shook hands and parted without Dannie realizing that he had told all he knew and learned nothing. Then he entered the post office for the weekly mail. He called for Malone's papers also, and with them came a slip from the express office notifying Jimmy that there was a package for him. Dannie went to see if they would let him have it, and as Jimmy lived in the country, and as he and Dannie were known to be partners, he was allowed to sign the book, and carry away a long, slender, wooden box, with a Boston tag. The Thread Man had sent Jimmy a present, and from the appearance of the box, Dannie made up his mind that it was a cane.

Straightway he drove home at a scandalous rate of speed, and on the way, he dressed Jimmy in a broadcloth suit, patent leathers, and a silk hat. Then he took him to a gold cure, where he learned to abhor whiskey in a week, and then to the priest, to whom he confessed that he had lied about the number of coons in the Canoper. And so peace brooded in Rainbow Bottom, and all of them were happy again. For with the passing of summer, Dannie had learned that heretofore there had been happiness of a sort, for them, and that if they could all get back to the old footing it would be well, or at least far better than it was at present. With Mary's tongue dripping gall, and her sweet face souring, and Jimmy hearing devils, no wonder poor Dannie overheated his team in a race to carry a package that promised to furnish some diversion.

Jimmy and Mary heard the racket, and standing on the celery hill, they saw Dannie come clattering up the lane, and as he saw them, he stood in the wagon, and waved the package over his head.

Jimmy straightened with a flourish, stuck the spade in the celery hill, and descended with great deliberation. "I mintioned to Dannie this morning," he said "that it was about time I was hearin' from the Thrid Man."

"Oh! Do you suppose it is something from Boston?" the eagerness in Mary's voice made it sound almost girlish again.

"Hunt the hatchet!" hissed Jimmy, and walked very leisurely into the cabin.

Dannie was visibly excited as he entered. "I think ye have heard from the Thread Mon," he said, handing Jimmy the package.

Jimmy took it, and examined it carefully. He never before in his life had an express package, the contents of which he did not know. It behooved him to get all there was out of the pride and the joy of it.

Mary laid down the hatchet so close that it touched Jimmy's hand, to remind him. "Now what do you suppose he has sent you?" she inquired eagerly, her hand straying toward the packages.

Jimmy tested the box. "It don't weigh much," he said, "but one end of it's the heaviest."

He set the hatchet in a tiny crack, and with one rip, stripped off the cover.

Inside lay a long, brown leather case, with small buckles, and in one end a little leather case, flat on one side, rounding on the other, and it, too, fastened with a buckle. Jimmy caught sight of a paper book folded in the bottom of the box, as he lifted the case. With trembling fingers he unfastened the buckles, the whole thing unrolled, and disclosed a case of leather, sewn in four divisions, from top to bottom, and from the largest of these protruded a shining object. Jimmy caught this, and began to draw, and the shine began to lengthen.

"Just what I thought!" exclaimed Dannie. "He's sent ye a fine cane."

"A hint to kape out of the small of his back the nixt time he goes promenadin' on a cow-kitcher! The divil!" exploded Jimmy.

His quick eyes had caught a word on the cover of the little book in the bottom of the box.

"A cane! A cane! Look at that, will ye?" He flashed six inches of grooved silvery handle before their faces, and three feet of shining black steel, scarcely thicker than a lead pencil. "Cane!" he cried scornfully. Then he picked up the box, and opening it drew out a little machine that shone like a silver watch, and setting it against the handle, slipped a small slide over each end, and it held firmly, and shone bravely.

"Oh, Jimmy, what is it?" cried Mary.

"Me cane!" answered Jimmy. "Me new cane from Boston. Didn't you hear Dannie sayin' what it was? This little arrangemint is my cicly-meter, like they put on wheels, and buggies now, to tell how far you've traveled. The way this works, I just tie this silk thrid to me door knob and off I walks, it a reeling out behind, and whin I turn back it takes up as I come, and whin I get home I take the yardstick and measure me string, and be the same token, it tells me how far I've traveled." As he talked he drew out another shining length and added it to the first, and then another and a last, fine as a wheat straw. "These last jints I'm adding," he explained to Mary, "are so that if I have me cane whin I'm riding I can stritch it out and touch up me horses with it. And betimes, if I should iver break me old cane fish pole, I could take this down to the river, and there, the books call it 'whipping the water.' See! Cane, be Jasus! It's the Jim-dandiest little fishing rod anybody in these parts iver set eyes on. Lord! What a beauty!"

He turned to Dannie and shook the shining, slender thing before his envious eyes.

"Who gets the Black Bass now?" he triumphed in tones of utter conviction.

There is no use in taking time to explain to any fisherman who has read thus far that Dannie, the patient; Dannie, the long-suffering, felt abused. How would you feel yourself?

"The Thread Man might have sent twa," was his thought. "The only decent treatment he got that nicht was frae me, and if I'd let Jimmy hit him, he'd gone through the wall. But there never is anything fra me!"

And that was true. There never was.

Aloud he said, "Dinna bother to hunt the steelyards, Mary. We winna weigh it until he brings it home."

"Yes, and by gum, I'll bring it with this! Look, here is a picture of a man in a boat, pullin' in a whale with a pole just like this," bragged Jimmy.

"Yes," said Dannie. "That's what it's made for. A boat and open water. If ye are going to fish wi' that thing along the river we'll have to cut doon all the trees, and that will dry up the water. That's na for river fishing."

Jimmy was intently studying the book. Mary tried to take the rod from his hand.

"Let be!" he cried, hanging on. "You'll break it!"

"I guess steel don't break so easy," she said aggrievedly. "I just wanted to 'heft' it."

"Light as a feather," boasted Jimmy. "Fish all day and it won't tire a man at all. Done—unjoint it and put it in its case, and not go dragging up everything along the bank like a living stump-puller. This book says this line will bear twinty pounds pressure, and sometimes it's takin' an hour to tire out a fish, if it's a fighter. I bet you the Black Bass is a fighter, from what we know of him."

"Ye can watch me land him and see what ye think about it," suggested Dannie.

Jimmy held the book with one hand and lightly waved the rod with the other, in a way that would have developed nerves in an Indian. He laughed absently.

"With me shootin' bait all over his pool with.this?" he asked. "I guess not!"

"But you can't fish for the Bass with that, Jimmy Malone," cried Mary hotly. "You agreed to fish fair for the Bass, and it wouldn't be fair for you to use that, whin Dannie only has his old cane pole. Dannie, get you a steel pole, too," she begged.

"If Jimmy is going to fish with that, there will be all the more glory in taking the Bass from him with the pole I have," answered Dannie.

"You keep out," cried Jimmy angrily to Mary. "It was a fair bargain. He made it himself. Each man was to fish surface or deep, and with his own pole and bait. I guess this IS my pole, ain't it?"

"Yes," said Mary. "But it wasn't yours whin you made that agreemint. You very well know Dannie expected you to fish with the same kind of pole and bait that he did; didn't you, Dannie?"

"Yes," said Dannie, "I did. Because I never dreamed of him havin' any other. But since he has it, I think he's in his rights if he fishes with it. I dinna care. In the first place he will only scare the Bass away from him with the racket that reel will make, and in the second, if he tries to land it with that thing, he will smash it, and lose the fish. There's a longhandled net to land things with that goes with those rods. He'd better sent ye one. Now you'll have to jump into the river and land a fish by hand if ye hook it."

"That's true!" cried Mary. "Here's one in a picture."

She had snatched the book from Jimmy. He snatched it back.

"Be careful, you'll tear that!" he cried. "I was just going to say that I would get some fine wire or mosquito bar and make one."

Dannie's fingers were itching to take the rod, if only for an instant. He looked at it longingly. But Jimmy was impervious. He whipped it softly about and eagerly read from the book.

"Tells here about a man takin' a fish that weighed forty pounds with a pole just like this," he announced. "Scat! Jumpin' Jehosophat! What do you think of that!"

"Couldn't you fish turn about with it?" inquired Mary.

"Na, we couldna fish turn about with it," answered Dannie. "Na with that pole. Jimmy would throw a fit if anybody else touched it. And he's welcome to it. He never in this world will catch the Black Bass with it. If I only had some way to put juist fifteen feet more line on my pole, I'd show him how to take the Bass to-morrow. The way we always have come to lose it is with too short lines. We have to try to land it before it's tired out and it's strong enough to break and tear away. It must have ragged jaws and a dozen pieces of line hanging to it, fra both of us have hooked it time and again. When it strikes me, if I only could give it fifteen feet more line, I could land it."

"Can't you fix some way?" asked Mary.

"I'll try," answered Dannie.

"And in the manetime, I'd just be givin' it twenty off me dandy little reel, and away goes me with Mr. Bass," said Jimmy. "I must take it to town and have its picture took to sind the Thrid Man."

And that was the last straw. Dannie had given up being allowed to touch the rod, and was on his way to unhitch his team and do the evening work. The day had been trying and just for the moment he forgot everything save that his longing fingers had not touched that beautiful little fishing rod.

"The Boston man forgot another thing," he said. "The Dude who shindys 'round with those things in pictures, wears a damn, dinky, little pleated coat!"

Chapter VIII

WHEN THE BLACK BASS STRUCK

"Lots of fish down in the brook,
All you need is a rod, and a line, and a hook,"

Hummed Jimmy, still lovingly fingering his possessions.

"Did Dannie iver say a thing like that to you before?" asked Mary.

"Oh, he's dead sore," explained Jimmy. "He thinks he should have had a jinted rod, too."

"And so he had," replied Mary. "You said yoursilf that you might have killed that man if Dannie hadn't showed you that you were wrong."

"You must think stuff like this is got at the tin-cint store," said Jimmy.

"Oh, no I don't!" said Mary. "I expect it cost three or four dollars."

"Three or four dollars," sneered Jimmy. "All the sinse a woman has! Feast your eyes on this book and rade that just this little reel alone cost fifteen, and there's no telling what the rod is worth. Why it's turned right out of pure steel, same as if it were wood. Look for yoursilf."

"Thanks, no! I'm afraid to touch it," said Mary.

"Oh, you are sore too!" laughed Jimmy. "With all that money in it, I should think you could see why I wouldn't want it broke."

"You've sat there and whipped it around for an hour. Would it break it for me or Dannie to do the same thing? If it had been his, you'd have had a worm on it and been down to the river trying it for him by now."

"Worm!" scoffed Jimmy. "A worm! That's a good one! Idjit! You don't fish with worms with a jinted rod."

"Well what do you fish with? Humming birds?"

"No. You fish with—" Jimmy stopped and eyed Mary dubiously. "You fish with a lot of things," he continued. "Some of thim come in little books and they look like moths, and some like snake-faders, and some of them are buck-tail and bits of tin, painted to look shiny. Once there was a man in town who had a minnie made of rubber and all painted up just like life. There were hooks on its head, and on its back, and its belly, and its tail, so's that if a fish snapped at it anywhere it got hooked."

"I should say so!" exclaimed Mary. "It's no fair way to fish, to use more than one hook. You might just as well take a net and wade in and seine out the fish as to take a lot of hooks and rake thim out."

"Well, who's going to take a lot of hooks and rake thim out?"

"I didn't say anybody was. I was just saying it wouldn't be fair to the fish if they did."

"Course I wouldn't fish with no riggin' like that, when Dannie only has one old hook. Whin we fish for the Bass, I won't use but one hook either. All the same, I'm going to have some of those fancy baits. I'm going to get Jim Skeels at the drug store to order thim for me. I know just how you do," said Jimmy flourishing the rod. "You put on your bait and quite a heavy sinker, and you wind it up to the ind of your rod, and thin you stand up in your boat——"

"Stand up in your boat!"

"I wish you'd let me finish!—or on the bank, and you take this little whipper-snapper, and you touch the spot on the reel that relases the thrid, and you give the rod a little toss, aisy as throwin' away chips, and off maybe fifty feet your bait hits the water, 'spat!' and 'snap!' goes Mr. Bass, and 'stick!' goes the hook. See?"

"What I see is that if you want to fish that way in the Wabash, you'll have to wait until the dredge goes through and they make a canal out of it; for be the time you'd throwed fifty feet, and your fish had run another fifty, there'd be just one hundred snags, and logs, and stumps between you; one for every foot of the way. It must look pretty on deep water, where it can be done right, but I bet anything that if you go to fooling with that on our river, Dannie gets the Bass."

"Not much, Dannie don't 'gets the Bass,'" said Jimmy confidently. "Just you come out here and let me show you how this works. Now you see, I put me sinker on the ind of the thrid, no hook of course, for practice, and I touch this little spring here, and give me little rod a whip and away goes me bait, slick as grase. Mr. Bass is layin' in thim bass weeds right out there, foreninst the pie-plant bed, and the bait strikes the water at the idge, see! and 'snap,' he takes it and sails off slow, to swally it at leisure. Here's where I don't pull a morsel. Jist let him rin and swally, and whin me line is well out and he has me bait all digistid, 'yank,' I give him the round-up, and THIN, the fun begins. He leps clear of the water and I see he's tin pound. If he rins from me, I give him rope, and if he rins to, I dig in, workin' me little machane for dear life to take up the thrid before it slacks. Whin he sees me, he makes a dash back, and I just got to relase me line and let him go, because he'd bust this little silk thrid all to thunder if I tried to force him onpleasant to his intintions, and so we kape it up until he's plum wore out and comes a promenadin' up to me boat, bank I mane, and I scoops him in, and that's sport, Mary! That's MAN'S fishin'! Now watch! He's in thim bass weeds before the pie-plant, like I said, and I'm here on the bank, and I THINK he's there, so I give me little jinted rod a whip and a swing——"

Jimmy gave the rod a whip and a swing. The sinker shot in air, struck the limb of an apple tree and wound a dozen times around it. Jimmy said things and Mary giggled. She also noticed that Dannie had stopped work and was standing in the barn door watching intently. Jimmy climbed the tree, unwound the line and tried again.

"I didn't notice that domn apple limb stickin' out there," he said. "Now you watch! Right out there among the bass weeds foreninst the pie-plant"

To avoid another limb, Jimmy aimed too low and the sinker shot under the well platform not ten feet from him.

"Lucky you didn't get fast in the bass weeds," said Mary as Jimmy reeled in.

"Will, I got to get me range," explained Jimmy. "This time——"

Jimmy swung too high. The spring slipped from under his unaccustomed thumb. The sinker shot above and behind him and became entangled in the eaves, while yards of the fine silk line flew off the spinning reel and dropped in tangled masses at his feet, and in an effort to do something Jimmy reversed the reel and it wound back on tangles and all until it became completely clogged. Mary had sat down on the back steps to watch the exhibition. Now, she stood up to laugh.

"And THAT'S just what will happen to you at the river," she said. "While you are foolin' with that thing, which ain't for rivers, and which you don't know beans about handlin', Dannie will haul in the Bass, and serve you right, too!"

"Mary," said Jimmy, "I niver struck ye in all me life, but if ye don't go in the house, and shut up, I'll knock the head off ye!"

"I wouldn't be advisin' you to," she said. "Dannie is watching you."

Jimmy glanced toward the barn in time to see Dannie's shaking shoulders as he turned from the door. With unexpected patience, he firmly closed his lips and went after a ladder. By the time he had the sinker loose and the line untangled, supper was ready. By the time he had mastered the reel, and could land the sinker accurately in front of various imaginary beds of bass weeds, Dannie had finished the night work in both stables and gone home. But his back door stood open and therefrom there protruded the point of a long, heavy cane fish pole. By the light of a lamp on his table, Dannie could be seen working with pincers and a ball of wire.

"I wonder what he thinks he can do?" said Jimmy.

"I suppose he is trying to fix some way to get that fifteen feet more line he needs," replied Mary.

When they went to bed the light still burned and the broad shoulders of Dannie bent over the pole. Mary had fallen asleep, but she was awakened by Jimmy slipping from the bed. He went to the window and looked toward Dannie's cabin. Then he left the bedroom and she could hear him crossing to the back window of the next room. Then came a smothered laugh and he softly called her. She went to him.

Dannie's figure stood out clear and strong in the moonlight, in his wood-yard. His black outline looked unusually powerful in the silvery whiteness surrounding it.

He held his fishing pole in both hands and swept a circle about him that would have required considerable space on Lake Michigan, and made a cast toward the barn. The line ran out smoothly and evenly, and through the gloom Mary saw Jimmy's figure straighten and his lips close in surprise. Then Dannie began taking in line. That process was so slow, Jimmy doubled up and laughed again.

"Be lookin' at that, will ye?" he heaved. "What does the domn fool think the Black Bass will be doin' while he is takin' in line on that young windlass?"

"There'd be no room on the river to do that," answered Mary serenely. "Dannie wouldn't be so foolish as to try. All he wants now is to see if his line will run, and it will. Whin he gets to the river, he'll swing his bait where he wants it with his pole, like he always does, and whin the Bass strikes he'll give it the extra fifteen feet more line he said he needed, and thin he'll have a pole and line with which he can land it."

"Not on your life he won't!" said Jimmy.

He opened the back door and stepped out just as Dannie raised the pole again.

"Hey, you! Quit raisin' Cain out there!" yelled Jimmy. "I want to get some sleep."

Across the night, tinged neither with chagrin nor rancor, boomed the big voice of Dannie.

"Believe I have my extra line fixed so it works all right," he said. "Awful sorry if I waked you. Thought I was quiet."

"How much did you make off that?" inquired Mary.

"Two points," answered Jimmy. "Found out that Dannie ain't sore at me any longer and that you are."

Next morning was no sort of angler's weather, but the afternoon gave promise of being good fishing by the morrow. Dannie worked about the farms, preparing for winter; Jimmy worked with him until mid-afternoon, then he hailed a boy passing, and they went away together. At supper time Jimmy had not returned. Mary came to where Dannie worked.

"Where's Jimmy?" she asked.

"I dinna, know" said Dannie. "He went away a while ago with some boy, I didna notice who."

"And he didn't tell you where he was going?"

"No."

"And he didn't take either of his fish poles?"

"No."

Mary's lips thinned to a mere line. "Then it's Casey's," she said, and turned away.

Dannie was silent. Presently Mary came back.

"If Jimmy don't come till morning," she asked, "or comes in shape that he can't fish, will you go without him?"

"To-morrow was the day we agreed on," answered Dannie.

"Will you go without him?" persisted Mary.

"What would HE do if it were me?" asked Dannie.

"When have you iver done to Jimmy Malone what he would do if he were you?"

"Is there any reason why ye na want me to land the Black Bass, Mary?"

"There is a particular reason why I don't want your living with Jimmy to make you like him," answered Mary. "My timper is being wined, and I can see where it's beginning to show on you. Whativer you do, don't do what he would."

"Dinna be hard on him, Mary. He doesna think," urged Dannie.

"You niver said twer words. He don't think. He niver thought about anybody in his life except himself, and he niver will."

"Maybe he didna go to town!"

"Maybe the sun won't rise in the morning, and it will always be dark after this! Come in and get your supper."

"I'd best pick up something to eat at home," said Dannie.

"I have some good food cooked, and it's a pity to be throwin' it away. What's the use? You've done a long day's work, more for us than yoursilf, as usual; come along and get your supper."

Dannie went, and as he was washing at the back door, Jimmy came through the barn, and up the walk. He was fresh, and in fine spirits, and where ever he had been, it was a sure thing that it was nowhere near Casey's.

"Where have you been?" asked Mary wonderingly.

"Robbin' graves," answered Jimmy promptly. "I needed a few stiffs in me business so I just went out to Five Mile and got them."

"What are ye going to do with them, Jimmy?" chuckled Dannie.

"Use thim for Bass bait! Now rattle, old snake!" replied Jimmy.

After supper Dannie went to the barn for the shovel to dig worms for bait, and noticed that Jimmy's rubber waders hanging on the wall were covered almost to the top with fresh mud and water stains, and Dannie's wonder grew.

Early the next morning they started for the river. As usual Jimmy led the way. He proudly carried his new rod. Dannie followed with a basket of lunch Mary had insisted on packing, his big cane pole, a can of worms, and a shovel, in case they ran out of bait.

Dannie had recovered his temper, and was just great-hearted, big Dannie again. He talked about the south wind, and shivered with the frost, and listened for the splash of the Bass. Jimmy had little to say. He seemed to be thinking deeply. No doubt he felt in his soul that they should settle the question of who landed the Bass with the same rods they had used when the contest was proposed, and that was not all.

When they came to the temporary bridge, Jimmy started across it, and Dannie called to him to wait, he was forgetting his worms.

"I don't want any worms," answered Jimmy briefly. He walked on. Dannie stood staring after him, for he did not understand that. Then he went slowly to his side of the river, and deposited his load under a tree where it would be out of the way.

He lay down his pole, took a rude wooden spool of heavy fish cord from his pocket, and passed the line through the loop next the handle and so on the length of the rod to the point. Then he wired on a sharp bass hook, and wound the wire far up the doubled line. As he worked, he kept an eye on Jimmy. He was doing practically the same thing. But just as Dannie had fastened on a light lead to carry his line, a souse in the river opposite attracted his attention. Jimmy hauled from the water a minnow bucket, and opening it, took out a live minnow, and placed it on his hook. "Riddy," he called, as he resank the bucket, and stood on the bank, holding his line in his fingers, and watching the minnow play at his feet.

The fact that Dannie was a Scotchman, and unusually slow and patient, did not alter the fact that he was just a common human being. The lump that rose in his throat was so big, and so hard, he did not try to swallow it. He hurried back into Rainbow Bottom. The first log he came across he kicked over, and grovelling in the rotten wood and loose earth with his hands, he brought up a half dozen bluish-white grubs. He tore up the ground for the length of the log, and then he went to others, cramming the worms and dirt with them into his pockets. When he had enough, he went back, and with extreme care placed three of them on his hook. He tried to see how Jimmy was going to fish, but he could not tell.

So Dannie decided that he would cast in the morning, fish deep at noon, and cast again toward evening.

He rose, turned to the river, and lifted his rod. As he stood looking over the channel, and the pool where the Bass homed, the Kingfisher came rattling down the river, and as if in answer to its cry, the Black Bass gave a leap, that sent the water flying.

"Ready!" cried Dannie, swinging his pole over the water.

As the word left his lips, "whizz," Jimmy's minnow landed in the middle of the circles widening about the rise of the Bass. There was a rush and a snap, and Dannie saw the jaws of the big fellow close within an inch of the minnow, and he swam after it for a yard, as Jimmy slowly reeled in. Dannie waited a second, and then softly dropped his grubs on the water just before where he figured the Bass would be. He could hear Jimmy smothering oaths. Dannie said something himself as his untouched bait neared the bank. He lifted it, swung it out, and slowly trailed it in again. "Spat!" came Jimmy's minnow almost at his feet, and again the Bass leaped for it. Again he missed. As the minnow reeled away the second time, Dannie swung his grubs higher, and struck the water "Spat," as the minnow had done. "Snap," went the Bass. One instant the line strained, the next the hook came up stripped clean of bait.

Then Dannie and Jimmy really went at it, and they were strangers. Not a word of friendly banter crossed the river. They cast until the Bass grew suspicious, and would not rise to the bait; then they fished deep. Then they cast again. If Jimmy fell into trouble with his reel, Dannie had the honesty to stop fishing until it worked again, but he spent the time burrowing for grubs until his hands resembled the claws of an animal. Sometimes they sat, and still- fished. Sometimes, they warily slipped along the bank, trailing bait a few inches under water. Then they would cast and skitter by turns.

The Kingfisher struck his stump, and tilted on again. His mate, and their family of six followed in his lead, so that their rattle was almost constant. A fussy little red-eyed vireo asked questions, first of Jimmy, and then crossing the river besieged Dannie, but neither of the stern-faced fishermen paid it any heed. The blackbirds swung on the rushes, and talked over the season. As always, a few crows cawed above the deep woods, and the chewinks threshed about among the dry leaves. A band of larks were gathering for migration, and the frosty air was vibrant with their calls to each other.

Killdeers were circling above them in flocks. A half dozen robins gathered over a wild grapevine, and chirped cheerfully, as they pecked at the frosted fruit. At times, the pointed nose of a muskrat wove its way across the river, leaving a shining ripple in its wake. In the deep woods squirrels barked and chattered. Frost-loosened crimson leaves came whirling down, settling in a bright blanket that covered the water several feet from the bank, and unfortunate bees that had fallen into the river struggled frantically to gain a footing on them. Water beetles shot over the surface in small shining parties, and schools of tiny minnows played along the banks. Once a black ant assassinated an enemy on Dannie's shoe, by creeping up behind it and puncturing its abdomen.

Noon came, and neither of the fishermen spoke or moved from their work. The lunch Mary had prepared with such care they had forgotten. A little after noon, Dannie got another strike, deep fishing. Mid-afternoon found them still even, and patiently fishing. Then it was not so long until supper time, and the air was steadily growing colder. The south wind had veered to the west, and signs of a black frost were in the air. About this time the larks arose as with one accord, and with a whirr of wings that proved how large the flock was, they sailed straight south.

Jimmy hauled his minnow bucket from the river, poured the water from it, and picked his last minnow, a dead one, from the grass. Dannie was watching him, and rightly guessed that he would fish deep. So Dannie scooped the remaining dirt from his pockets, and found three grubs. He placed them on his hook, lightened his sinker, and prepared to skitter once more.

Jimmy dropped his minnow beside the Kingfisher stump, and let it sink. Dannie hit the water at the base of the stump, where it had not been disturbed for a long time, a sharp "Spat," with his worms. Something seized his bait, and was gone. Dannie planted his feet firmly, squared his jaws, gripped his rod, and loosened his line. As his eye followed it, he saw to his amazement that Jimmy's line was sailing off down the river beside his, and heard the reel singing.

Dannie was soon close to the end of his line. He threw his weight into a jerk enough to have torn the head from a fish, and down the river the Black Bass leaped clear of the water, doubled, and with a mighty shake tried to throw the hook from his mouth.

"Got him fast, by God!" screamed Jimmy in triumph.

Straight toward them rushed the fish. Jimmy reeled wildly; Dannie gathered in his line by yard lengths, and grasped it with the hand that held the rod. Near them the Bass leaped again, and sped back down the river. Jimmy's reel sang, and Dannie's line jerked through his fingers. Back came the fish. Again Dannie gathered in line, and Jimmy reeled frantically. Then Dannie, relying on the strength of his line thought he could land the fish, and steadily drew it toward him. Jimmy's reel began to sing louder, and his line followed Dannie's. Instantly Jimmy went wild.

"Stop pullin' me little silk thrid!" he yelled. "I've got the Black Bass hooked fast as a rock, and your domn clothes line is sawin' across me. Cut there! Cut that domn rope! Quick!"

"He's mine, and I'll land him!" roared Dannie. "Cut yoursel', and let me get my fish!"

So it happened, that when Mary Malone, tired of waiting for the boys to come, and anxious as to the day's outcome, slipped down to the Wabash to see what they were doing, she heard sounds that almost paralyzed her. Shaking with fear, she ran toward the river, and paused at a little thicket behind Dannie.

Jimmy danced and raged on the opposite bank. "Cut!" he yelled. "Cut that domn cable, and let me Bass loose! Cut your line, I say!"

Dannie stood with his feet planted wide apart, and his jaws set. He drew his line steadily toward him, and Jimmy's followed. "Ye see!" exulted Dannie. "Ye're across me. The Bass is mine! Reel out your line till I land him, if ye dinna want it broken."

"If you don't cut your domn line, I will!" raved Jimmy.

"Cut nothin'!" cried Dannie. "Let's see ye try to touch it!"

Into the river went Jimmy; splash went Dannie from his bank. He was nearer the tangled lines, but the water was deepest on his side, and the mud of the bed held his feet. Jimmy reached the crossed lines, knife in hand, by the time Dannie was there.

"Will you cut?" cried Jimmy.

"Na!" bellowed Dannie. "I've give up every damn thing to ye all my life, but I'll no give up the Black Bass. He's mine, and I'll land him!"

Jimmy made a lunge for the lines. Dannie swung his pole backward drawing them his way. Jimmy slashed again. Dannie dropped his pole, and with a sweep, caught the twisted lines in his fingers.

"Noo, let's see ye cut my line! Babby!" he jeered.

Jimmy's fist flew straight, and the blood streamed from Dannie's nose. Dannie dropped the lines, and straightened. "You—" he panted. "You—" And no other words came.

If Jimmy had been possessed of any small particle of reason, he lost it at the sight of blood on Dannie's face.

"You're a domn fish thief!" he screamed.

"Ye lie!" breathed Dannie, but his hand did not lift.

"You are a coward! You're afraid to strike like a man! Hit me! You don't dare hit me!"

"Ye lie!" repeated Dannie.

"You're a dog!" panted Jimmy. "I've used you to wait on me all me life!"

"THAT'S the God's truth!" cried Dannie. But he made no movement to strike. Jimmy leaned forward with a distorted, insane face.

"That time you sint me to Mary for you, I lied to her, and married her meself. NOW, will you fight like a man?"

Dannie made a spring, and Jimmy crumpled up in his grasp.

"Noo, I will choke the miserable tongue out of your heid, and twist the heid off your body, and tear the body to mince-meat," raved Dannie, and he promptly began the job.

With one awful effort Jimmy tore the gripping hands from his throat a little. "Lie!" he gasped. "It's all a lie!"

"It's the truth! Before God it's the truth!" Mary Malone tried to scream behind them. "It's the truth! It's the truth!" And her ears told her that she was making no sound as with dry lips she mouthed it over and over. And then she fainted, and sank down in the bushes.

Dannie's hands relaxed a little, he lifted the weight of Jimmy's body by his throat, and set him on his feet. "I'll give ye juist ane chance," he said. "IS THAT THE TRUTH?"

Jimmy's awful eyes were bulging from his head, his hands were clawing at Dannie's on his throat, and his swollen lips repeated it over and over as breath came, "It's a lie! It's a lie!"

"I think so myself," said Dannie. "Ye never would have dared. Ye'd have known that I'd find out some day, and on that day, I'd kill ye as I would a copperhead."

"A lie!" panted Jimmy.

"Then WHY did ye tell it?" And Dannie's fingers threatened to renew their grip.

"I thought if I could make you strike back," gasped Jimmy, "my hittin' you wouldn't same so bad."

Then Dannie's hands relaxed. "Oh, Jimmy! Jimmy!" he cried. "Was there ever any other mon like ye?"

Then he remembered the cause of their trouble.

"But, I'm everlastingly damned," Dannie went on, "if I'll gi'e up the Black Bass to ye, unless it's on your line. Get yourself up there on your bank!"

The shove he gave Jimmy almost upset him, and Jimmy waded back, and as he climbed the bank, Dannie was behind him. After him he dragged a tangled mass of lines and poles, and at the last up the bank, and on the grass, two big fish; one, the great Black Bass of Horseshoe Bend; and the other nearly as large, a channel catfish; undoubtedly, one of those which had escaped into the Wabash in an overflow of the Celina reservoir that spring.

"NOO, I'll cut," said Dannie. "Keep your eye on me sharp. See me cut my line at the end o' my pole." He snipped the line in two. "Noo watch," he cautioned, "I dinna want contra deection about this!"

He picked up the Bass, and taking the line by which it was fast at its mouth, he slowly drew it through his fingers. The wiry silk line slipped away, and the heavy cord whipped out free.

"Is this my line?" asked Dannie, holding it up.

Jimmy nodded.

"Is the Black Bass my fish? Speak up!" cried Dannie, dangling the fish from the line.

"It's yours," admitted Jimmy.

"Then I'll be damned if I dinna do what I please wi' my own!" cried Dannie. With trembling fingers he extracted the hook, and dropped it. He took the gasping big fish in both hands, and tested its weight. "Almost seex," he said. "Michty near seex!" And he tossed the Black Bass back into the Wabash.

Then he stooped, and gathered up his pole and line.

With one foot he kicked the catfish, the tangled silk line, and the jointed rod, toward Jimmy. "Take your fish!" he said. He turned and plunged into the river, recrossed it as he came, gathered up the dinner pail and shovel, passed Mary Malone, a tumbled heap in the bushes, and started toward his cabin.

The Black Bass struck the water with a splash, and sank to the mud of the bottom, where he lay joyfully soaking his dry gills, parched tongue, and glazed eyes. He scooped water with his tail, and poured it over his torn jaw. And then he said to his progeny, "Children, let this be a warning to you. Never rise to but one grub at a time. Three is too good to be true! There is always a stinger in their midst." And the Black Bass ruefully shook his sore head and scooped more water.

Chapter IX

WHEN JIMMY MALONE CAME TO CONFESSION

DANNIE never before had known such anger as possessed him when he trudged homeward across Rainbow Bottom. His brain whirled in a tumult of conflicting passions, and his heart pained worse than his swelling face. In one instant the knowledge that Jimmy had struck him, possessed him with a desire to turn back and do murder. In the next, a sense of profound scorn for the cowardly lie which had driven him to the rage that kills encompassed him, and then in a surge came compassion for Jimmy, at the remberence of the excuse he had offered for saying that thing. How childish! But how like Jimmy! What was the use in trying to deal with him as if he were a man? A great spoiled, selfish baby was all he ever would be.

The fallen leaves rustled about Dannie's feet. The blackbirds above him in chattering debate discussed migration. A stiff breeze swept the fields, topped the embankment, and rushed down circling about Dannie, and setting his teeth chattering, for he was almost as wet as if he had been completely immersed. As the chill struck in, from force of habit he thought of Jimmy. If he was ever going to learn how to take care of himself, a man past thirty-five should know. Would he come home and put on dry clothing? But when had Jimmy taken care of himself? Dannie felt that he should go back, bring him home, and make him dress quickly.

A sharp pain shot across Dannie's swollen face. His lips shut firmly. No! Jimmy had struck him. And Jimmy was in the wrong. The fish was his, and he had a right to it. No man living would have given it up to Jimmy, after he had changed poles. And slipped away with a boy and gotten those minnows, too! And wouldn't offer him even one. Much good they had done him. Caught a catfish on a dead one! Wonder if he would take the catfish to town and have its picture taken! Mighty fine fish, too, that channel cat! If it hadn't been for the Black Bass, they would have wondered and exclaimed over it, and carefully weighed it, and commented on the gamy fight it made. Just the same he was glad, that he landed the Bass. And he got it fairly. If Jimmy's old catfish mixed up with his line, he could not help that. He baited, hooked, played, and landed the Bass all right, and without any minnows either.

When he reached the top of the hill he realized that he was going to look back. In spite of Jimmy's selfishness, in spite of the blow, in spite of the ugly lie, Jimmy had been his lifelong partner, and his only friend, and stiffen his neck as he would, Dannie felt his head turning. He deliberately swung his fish pole into the bushes, and when it caught, as he knew it would, he set down his load, and turned as if to release it. Not a sight of Jimmy anywhere! Dannie started on.

"We are after you, Jimmy Malone!"

A thin, little, wiry thread of a cry, that seemed to come twisting as if wrung from the chill air about him, whispered in his ear, and Dannie jumped, dropped his load, and ran for the river. He couldn't see a sign of Jimmy. He hurried over the shaky little bridge they had built. The catfish lay gasping on the grass, the case and jointed rod lay on a log, but Jimmy was gone.

Dannie gave the catfish a shove that sent it well into the river, and ran for the shoals at the lower curve of Horseshoe Bend. The tracks of Jimmy's crossing were plain, and after him hurried Dannie. He ran up the hill, and as he reached the top he saw Jimmy climb on a wagon out on the road. Dannie called, but the farmer touched up his horses and trotted away without hearing him. "The fool! To ride!" thought Dannie. "Noo he will chill to the bone!".

Dannie cut across the fields to the lane and gathered up his load. With the knowledge that Jimmy had started for town came the thought of Mary. What was he going to say to her? He would have to make a clean breast of it, and he did not like the showing. In fact, he simply could not make a clean breast of it. Tell her? He could not tell her. He would lie to her once more, this one time for himself. He would tell her he fell in the river to account for his wet clothing and bruised face, and wait until Jimmy came home and see what he told her.

He went to the cabin and tapped at the door; there was no answer, so he opened it and set the lunch basket inside. Then he hurried home, built a fire, bathed, and put on dry clothing. He wondered where Mary was. He was ravenously hungry now. He did all the evening work, and as she still did not come, he concluded that she had gone to town, and that Jimmy knew she was there. Of course, that was it! Jimmy could get dry clothing of his brother-in-law. To be sure, Mary had gone to town. That was why Jimmy went.

And he was right. Mary had gone to town. When sense slowly returned to her she sat up in the bushes and stared about her. Then she arose and looked toward the river. The men were gone. Mary guessed the situation rightly. They were too much of river men to drown in a few feet of water; they scarcely would kill each other. They had fought, and Dannie had gone home, and Jimmy to the consolation of Casey's. WHERE SHOULD SHE GO? Mary Malone's lips set in a firm line.

"It's the truth! It's the truth!" she panted over and over, and now that there was no one to hear, she found that she could say it quite plainly. As the sense of her outraged womanhood swept over her she grew almost delirious. "I hope you killed him, Dannie Micnoun," she raved. "I hope you killed him, for if you didn't, I will. Oh! Oh!"

She was almost suffocating with rage. The only thing clear to her was that she never again would live an hour with Jimmy Malone. He might have gone home. Probably he did go for dry clothing. She would go to her sister. She hurried across the bottom, with wavering knees she climbed the embankment, then skirting the fields, she half walked, half ran to the village, and selecting back streets and alleys, tumbled, half distracted, into the home of her sister.

"Holy Vargin!" screamed Katy Dolan. "Whativer do be ailin' you, Mary Malone?"

"Jimmy! Jimmy!" sobbed the shivering Mary.

"I knew it! I knew it! I've ixpicted it for years!" cried Katy.

"They've had a fight——"

"Just what I looked for! I always told you they were too thick to last!"

"And Jimmy told Dannie he'd lied to me and married me himsilf——"

"He did! I saw him do it!" screamed Katy.

"And Dannie tried to kill him——"

"I hope to Hivin he got it done, for if any man iver naded killin'! A carpse named Jimmy Malone would a looked good to me any time these fiftane years. I always said——"

"And he took it back——"

"Just like the rid divil! I knew he'd do it! And of course that mutton-head of a Dannie Micnoun belaved him, whativer he said"

"Of course he did!"

"I knew it! Didn't I say so first?"

"And I tried to scrame and me tongue stuck——"

"Sure! You poor lamb! My tongue always sticks! Just what I ixpicted!"

"And me head just went round and I keeled over in the bushes——"

"I've told Dolan a thousand times! I knew it! It's no news to me!"

"And whin I came to, they were gone, and I don't know where, and I don't care! But I won't go back! I won't go back! I'll not live with him another day. Oh, Katy! Think how you'd feel if some one had siparated you and Dolan before you'd iver been togither!"

Katie Dolan gathered her sister into her arms. "You poor lamb," she wailed. "I've known ivery word of this for fiftane years, and if I'd had the laste idea 'twas so, I'd a busted Jimmy Malone to smithereens before it iver happened!"

"I won't go back! I won't go back!" raved Mary.

"I guess you won't go back," cried Katy, patting every available spot on Mary, or making dashes at her own eyes to stop the flow of tears. "I guess you won't go back! You'll stay right here with me. I've always wanted you! I always said I'd love to have you! I've told thim from the start there was something wrong out there! I've ixpicted you ivry day for years, and I niver was so surprised in all me life as whin you came! Now, don't you shed another tear. The Lord knows this is enough, for anybody. None at all would be too many for Jimmy Malone. You get right into bid, and I'll make you a cup of rid-pipper tay to take the chill out of you. And if Jimmy Malone comes around this house I'll lav him out with the poker, and if Dannie Micnoun comes saft-saddering after him I'll stritch him out too; yis, and if Dolan's got anything to say, he can take his midicine like the rist. The min are all of a pace anyhow! I've always said it! If I wouldn't like to get me fingers on that haythen; never goin' to confission, spindin' ivrything on himself you naded for dacent livin'! Lit him come! Just lit him come!"

Thus forestalled with knowledge, and overwhelmed with kindness, Mary Malone cuddled up in bed and sobbed herself to sleep, and Katy Dolan assured her, as long as she was conscious, that she always had known it, and if Jimmy Malone came near, she had the poker ready.

Dannie did the evening work. When he milked he drank most of it, but that only made him hungrier, so he ate the lunch he had brought back from the river, as he sat before a roaring fire. His heart warmed with his body. Irresponsible Jimmy always had aroused something of the paternal instinct in Dannie. Some one had to be responsible, so Dannie had been. Some way he felt responsible now. With another man like himself, it would have been man to man, but he always had spoiled Jimmy; now who was to blame that he was spoiled?

Dannie was very tired, his face throbbed and ached painfully, and it was a sight to see. His bed never had looked so inviting, and never had the chance to sleep been further away. With a sigh, he buttoned his coat, twisted an old scarf around his neck, and started for the barn. There was going to be a black frost. The cold seemed to pierce him. He hitched to the single buggy, and drove to town. He went to Casey's, and asked for Jimmy.

"He isn't here," said Casey.

"Has he been here?" asked Dannie.

Casey hesitated, and then blurted out, "He said you wasn't his keeper, and if you came after him, to tell you to go to Hell."

Then Dannie was sure that Jimmy was in the back room, drying his clothing. So he drove to Mrs. Dolan's, and asked if Mary were there for the night. Mrs. Dolan said she was, and she was going to stay, and he might tell Jimmy Malone that he need not come near them, unless he wanted his head laid open. She shut the door forcibly.

Dannie waited until Casey closed at eleven, and to his astonishment Jimmy was not among the men who came out. That meant that he had drank lightly after all, slipped from the back door, and gone home. And yet, would he do it, after what he had said about being afraid? If he had not drank heavily, he would not go into the night alone, when he had been afraid in the daytime. Dannie climbed from the buggy once more, and patiently searched the alley and the street leading to the footpath across farms. No Jimmy. Then Dannie drove home, stabled his horse, and tried Jimmy's back door. It was unlocked. If Jimmy were there, he probably would be lying across the bed in his clothing, and Dannie knew that Mary was in town. He made a light, and cautiously entered the sleeping room, intending to undress and cover Jimmy, but Jimmy was not there.

Dannie's mouth fell open. He put out the light, and stood on the back steps. The frost had settled in a silver sheen over the roofs of the barns and the sheds, and a scum of ice had frozen over a tub of drippings at the well. Dannie was bitterly cold. He went home, and hunted out his winter overcoat, lighted his lantern, picked up a heavy cudgel in the corner, and started to town on foot over the path that lay across the fields. He followed it to Casey's back door. He went to Mrs. Dolan's again, but everything was black and silent there. There had been evening trains. He thought of Jimmy's frequent threat to go away. He dismissed that thought grimly. There had been no talk of going away lately, and he knew that Jimmy had little money. Dannie started for home, and for a rod on either side he searched the path. As he came to the back of the barns, he rated himself for not thinking of them first. He searched both of them, and all around them, and then wholly tired, and greatly disgusted, he went home and to bed. He decided that Jimmy HAD gone to Mrs. Dolan's and that kindly woman had relented and taken him in. Of course that was where he was.

Dannie was up early in the morning. He wanted to have the work done before Mary and Jimmy came home. He fed the stock, milked, built a fire, and began cleaning the stables. As he wheeled the first barrow of manure to the heap, he noticed a rooster giving danger signals behind the straw-stack. At the second load it was still there, and Dannie went to see what alarmed it.

Jimmy lay behind the stack, where he had fallen face down, and as Dannie tried to lift him he saw that he would have to cut him loose, for he had frozen fast in the muck of the barnyard. He had pitched forward among the rough cattle and horse tracks and fallen within a few feet of the entrance to a deep hollow eaten out of the straw by the cattle. Had he reached that shelter he would have been warm enough and safe for the night.

Horrified, Dannie whipped out his knife, cut Jimmy's clothing loose and carried him to his bed. He covered him, and hitching up drove at top speed for a doctor. He sent the physician ahead and then rushed to Mrs. Dolan's. She saw him drive up and came to the door.

"Send Mary home and ye come too," Dannie called before she had time to speak. "Jimmy lay oot all last nicht, and I'm afraid he's dead."

Mrs. Dolan hurried in and repeated the message to Mary. She sat speechless while her sister bustled about putting on her wraps.

"I ain't goin'," she said shortly. "If I got sight of him, I'd kill him if he wasn't dead."

"Oh, yis you are goin'," said Katy Dolan. "If he's dead, you know, it will save you being hanged for killing him. Get on these things of mine and hurry. You got to go for decency sake; and kape a still tongue in your head. Dannie Micnoun is waiting for us."

Together they went out and climbed into the carriage. Mary said nothing, but Dannie was too miserable to notice.

"You didn't find him thin, last night?" asked Mrs. Dolan.

"Na!" shivered Dannie. "I was in town twice. I hunted almost all nicht. At last I made sure you had taken him in and I went to bed. It was three o'clock then. I must have passed often, wi'in a few yards of him."

"Where was he?" asked Katy.

"Behind the straw-stack," replied Dannie.

"Do you think he will die?"

"Dee!" cried Dannie. "Jimmy dee! Oh, my God! We mauna let him!"

Mrs. Dolan took a furtive peep at Mary, who, dry-eyed and white, was staring straight ahead. She was trembling and very pale, but if Katy Dolan knew anything she knew that her sister's face was unforgiving and she did not in the least blame her.

Dannie reached home as soon as the horse could take them, and under the doctor's directions all of them began work. Mary did what she was told, but she did it deliberately, and if Dannie had taken time to notice her he would have seen anything but his idea of a woman facing death for any one she ever had loved. Mary's hurt went so deep, Mrs. Dolan had trouble to keep it covered.

Some of the neighbors said Mary was cold-hearted, and some of them that she was stupefied with grief.

Without stopping for food or sleep, Dannie nursed Jimmy. He rubbed, he bathed, he poulticed, he badgered the doctor and cursed his inability to do some good. To every one except Dannie, Jimmy's case was hopeless from the first. He developed double pneumonia in its worst form and he was in no condition to endure it in the lightest. His labored breathing could be heard all over the cabin, and he could speak only in gasps. On the third day he seemed a little better, and when Dannie asked what he could do for him, "Father Michael," Jimmy panted, and clung to Dannie's hand.

Dannie sent a man and remained with Jimmy. He made no offer to go when the priest came.

"This is probably in the nature of a last confession," said Father Michael to Dannie, "I shall have to ask you to leave us alone."

Dannie felt the hand that clung to him relax, and the perspiration broke on his temples. "Shall I go, Jimmy?" he asked.

Jimmy nodded. Dannie arose heavily and left the room. He sat down outside the door and rested his head in his hands.

The priest stood beside Jimmy. "The doctor tells me it is difficult for you to speak," he said, "I will help you all I can. I will ask questions and you need only assent with your head or hand. Do you wish the last sacrament administered, Jimmy Malone?"

The sweat rolled off Jimmy's brow. He assented.

"Do you wish to make final confession?"

A great groan shook Jimmy. The priest remembered a gay, laughing boy, flinging back a shock of auburn hair, his feet twinkling in the lead of the dance. Here was ruin to make the heart of compassion ache. The Father bent and clasped the hand of Jimmy firmly. The question he asked was between Jimmy Malone and his God. The answer almost strangled him.

"Can you confess that mortal sin, Jimmy?" asked the priest.

The drops on Jimmy's face merged in one bath of agony. His hands clenched and his breath seemed to go no lower than his throat.

"Lied—Dannie," he rattled. "Sip-rate him—and Mary."

"Are you trying to confess that you betrayed a confidence of Dannie Macnoun and married the girl who belonged to him, yourself?"

Jimmy assented.

His horrified eyes hung on the priest's face and saw it turn cold and stern. Always the thing he had done had tormented him; but not until the past summer had he begun to realize the depth of it, and it had almost unseated his reason. But not until now had come fullest appreciation, and Jimmy read it in the eyes filled with repulsion above him.

"And with that sin on your soul, you ask the last sacrament and the seal of forgiveness! You have not wronged God and the Holy Catholic Church as you have this man, with whom you have lived for years, while you possessed his rightful wife. Now he is here, in deathless devotion, fighting to save you. You may confess to him. If he will forgive you, God and the Church will ratify it, and set the seal on your brow. If not, you die unshriven! I will call Dannie Macnoun."

One gurgling howl broke from the swollen lips of Jimmy.

As Dannie entered the room, the priest spoke a few words to him, stepped out and closed the door. Dannie hurried to Jimmy's side.

"He said ye wanted to tell me something," said Dannie. "What is it? Do you want me to do anything for you?"

Suddenly Jimmy struggled to a sitting posture. His popping eyes almost burst from their sockets as he clutched Dannie with both hands. The perspiration poured in little streams down his dreadful face.

"Mary," the next word was lost in a strangled gasp. Then came "yours" and then a queer rattle. Something seemed to give way. "The Divils!" he shrieked. "The Divils have got me!"

Snap! his heart failed, and Jimmy Malone went out to face his record, unforgiven by man, and unshriven by priest.

Chapter X

DANNIE'S RENUNCIATION

SO they stretched Jimmy's length on Five Mile Hill beside the three babies that had lacked the "vital spark." Mary went to the Dolans for the winter and Dannie was left, sole occupant of Rainbow Bottom. Because so much fruit and food that would freeze were stored there, he was even asked to live in Jimmy's cabin.

Dannie began the winter stolidly. All day long and as far as he could find anything to do in the night, he worked. He mended everything about both farms, rebuilt all the fences and as a never-failing resource, he cut wood. He cut so much that he began to realize that it would get too dry and the burning of it would become extravagant, so he stopped that and began making some changes he had long contemplated. During fur time he set his line of traps on his side of the river and on the other he religiously set Jimmy's.

But he divided the proceeds from the skins exactly in half, no matter whose traps caught them, and with Jimmy's share of the money he started a bank account for Mary. As he could not use all of them he sold Jimmy's horses, cattle and pigs. With half the stock gone he needed only half the hay and grain stored for feeding. He disposed of the chickens, turkeys, ducks, and geese that Mary wanted sold, and placed the money to her credit. He sent her a beautiful little red bank book and an explanation of all these transactions by Dolan. Mary threw the book across the room because she wanted Dannie to keep her money himself, and then cried herself to sleep that night, because Dannie had sent the book instead of bringing it. But when she fully understood the transactions and realized that if she chose she could spend several hundred dollars, she grew very proud of that book.

About the empty cabins and the barns, working on the farms, wading the mud and water of the river bank, or tingling with cold on the ice went two Dannies. The one a dull, listless man, mechanically forcing a tired, overworked body to action, and the other a self- accused murderer.

"I am responsible for the whole thing," he told himself many times a day. "I always humored Jimmy. I always took the muddy side of the road, and the big end of the log, and the hard part of the work, and filled his traps wi' rats from my own; why in God's name did I let the Deil o' stubbornness in me drive him to his death. noo? Why didna I let him have the Black Bass? Why didna I make him come home and put on dry clothes? I killed him, juist as sure as if I'd taken an ax and broken his heid."

Through every minute of the exposure of winter outdoors and the torment of it inside, Dannie tortured himself. Of Mary he seldom thought at all. She was safe with her sister, and although Dannie did not know when or how it happened, he awoke one day to the realization that he had renounced her. He had killed Jimmy; he could not take his wife and his farm. And Dannie was so numb with long-suffering, that he did not much care. There come times when troubles pile so deep that the edge of human feeling is dulled.

He would take care of Mary, yes, she was as much Jimmy's as his farm, but he did not want her for himself now. If he had to kill his only friend, he would not complete his downfall by trying to win his wife. So through that winter Mary got very little consideration in the remorseful soul of Dannie, and Jimmy grew, as the dead grow, by leaps and bounds, until by spring Dannie had him well-nigh canonized.

When winter broke, Dannie had his future well mapped out. And that future was devotion to Jimmy's memory, with no more of Mary in it than was possible to keep out. He told himself that he was glad she was away and he did not care to have her return. Deep in his soul he harbored the feeling that he had killed Jimmy to make himself look victor in her eyes in such a small matter as taking a fish. And deeper yet a feeling that, everything considered, still she might mourn Jimmy more than she did.

So Dannie definitely settled that he always would live alone on the farms. Mary should remain with her sister, and at his death, everything should be hers. The night he finally reached that decision, the Kingfisher came home. Dannie heard his rattle of exultation as he struck the embankment and the suffering man turned his face to the wall and sobbed aloud, so that for a little time he stifled Jimmy's dying gasps that in wakeful night hours sounded in his ears. Early the next morning he drove through the village on his way to the county seat, with a load of grain. Dolan saw him and running home he told Mary. "He will be gone all day. Now is your chance!" he said.

Mary sprang to her feet, "Hurry!" she panted, "hurry!"

An hour later a loaded wagon, a man and three women drew up before the cabins in Rainbow Bottom. Mary, her sister, Dolan, and a scrub woman entered. Mary pointed out the objects which she wished removed, and Dolan carried them out. They took up the carpets, swept down the walls, and washed the windows. They hung pictures, prints, and lithographs, and curtained the windows in dainty white. They covered the floors with bright carpets, and placed new ornaments on the mantle, and comfortable furniture in the rooms. There was a white iron bed, and several rocking chairs, and a shelf across the window filled with potted hyacinths in bloom. Among them stood a glass bowl, containing three wonderful little gold fish, and from the top casing hung a brass cage, from which a green linnet sang an exultant song.

You should have seen Mary Malone! When everything was finished, she was changed the most of all. She was so sure of Dannie, that while the winter had brought annoyance that he did not come, it really had been one long, glorious rest. She laughed and sang, and grew younger with every passing day. As youth surged back, with it returned roundness of form, freshness of face, and that bred the desire to be daintily dressed. So of pretty light fabrics she made many summer dresses, for wear mourning she would not.

When calmness returned to Mary, she had told the Dolans the whole story. "Now do you ixpict me to grieve for the man?" she asked. "Fiftane years with him, through his lying tongue, whin by ivery right of our souls and our bodies, Dannie Micnoun and I belanged to each other. Mourn for him! I'm glad he's dead! Glad! Glad! If he had not died, I should have killed him, if Dannie did not! It was a happy thing that he died. His death saved me mortal sin. I'm glad, I tell you, and I do not forgive him, and I niver will, and I hope he will burn——"

Katy Dolan clapped her hand over Mary's mouth. "For the love of marcy, don't say that!" she cried. "You will have to confiss it, and you'd be ashamed to face the praste."

"I would not," cried Mary. "Father Michael knows I'm just an ordinary woman, he don't ixpict me to be an angel." But she left the sentence unfinished.

After Mary's cabin was arranged to her satisfaction, they attacked Dannie's; emptying it, cleaning it completely, and refurnishing it from the best of the things that had been in both. Then Mary added some new touches. A comfortable big chair was placed by his fire, new books on his mantle, a flower in his window, and new covers on his bed. While the women worked, Dolan raked the yards, and freshened matters outside as best he could. When everything they had planned to do was accomplished, the wagon, loaded with the ugly old things Mary despised, drove back to the village, and she, with little Tilly Dolan for company, remained.

Mary was tense with excitement. All the woman in her had yearned for these few pretty things she wanted for her home throughout the years that she had been compelled to live in crude, ugly surroundings; because every cent above plainest clothing and food, went for drink for Jimmy, and treats for his friends. Now she danced and sang, and flew about trying a chair here, and another there, to get the best effect. Every little while she slipped into her bedroom, stood before a real dresser, and pulled out its trays to make sure that her fresh, light dresses were really there. She shook out the dainty curtains repeatedly, watered the flowers, and fed the fish when they did not need it. She babbled incessantly to the green linnet, which with swollen throat rejoiced with her, and occasionally she looked in the mirror.

She lighted the fire, and put food to cook. She covered a new table, with a new cloth, and set it with new dishes, and placed a jar of her flowers in the center. What a supper she did cook! When she had waited until she was near crazed with nervousness, she heard the wagon coming up the lane. Peeping from the window, she saw Dannie stop the horses short, and sit staring at the cabins, and she realized that smoke would be curling from the chimney, and the flowers and curtains would change the shining windows outside. She trembled with excitement, and than a great yearning seized her, as he slowly drove closer, for his brown hair was almost white, and the lines on his face seemed indelibly stamped. And then hot anger shook her. Fifteen years of her life wrecked, and look at Dannie! That was Jimmy Malone's work.

Over and over, throughout the winter, she had planned this home- coming as a surprise to Dannie. Book-fine were the things she intended to say to him. When he opened the door, and stared at her and about the altered room, she swiftly went to him, and took the bundles he carried from his arms.

"Hurry up, and unhitch, Dannie," she said. "Your supper is waiting."

And Dannie turned and stolidly walked back to his team, without uttering a word.

"Uncle Dannie!" cried a child's voice. "Please let me ride to the barn with you!"

A winsome little maid came rushing to Dannie, threw her arms about his neck, and hugged him tight, as he stooped to lift her. Her yellow curls were against his cheek, and her breath was flower- sweet in his face.

"Why didn't you kiss Aunt Mary?" she demanded. "Daddy Dolan always kisses mammy when he comes from all day gone. Aunt Mary's worked so hard to please you. And Daddie worked, and mammy worked, and another woman. You are pleased, ain't you, Uncle Dannie?"

"Who told ye to call me Uncle?" asked Dannie, with unsteady lips.

"She did!" announced the little woman, flourishing the whip in the direction of the cabin. Dannie climbed down to unhitch. "You are goin' to be my Uncle, ain't you, as soon as it's a little over a year, so folks won't talk?"

"Who told ye that?" panted Dannie, hiding behind a horse.

"Nobody told me! Mammy just SAID it to Daddy, and I heard," answered the little maid. "And I'm glad of it, and so are all of us glad. Mammy said she'd just love to come here now, whin things would be like white folks. Mammy said Aunt Mary had suffered a lot more'n her share. Say, you won't make her suffer any more, will you?"

"No," moaned Dannie, and staggered into the barn with the horses. He leaned against a stall, and shut his eyes. He could see the bright room, plainer than ever, and that little singing bird sounded loud as any thunder in his ears. And whether closed or open, he could see Mary, never in all her life so beautiful, never so sweet; flesh and blood Mary, in a dainty dress, with the shining, unafraid eyes of girlhood. It was that thing which struck Dannie first, and hit him hardest. Mary was a careless girl again. When before had he seen her with neither trouble, anxiety or, worse yet, FEAR, in her beautiful eyes?

And she had come to stay. She would not have refurnished her cabin otherwise. Dannie took hold of the manger with both hands, because his sinking knees needed bracing.

"Dannie," called Mary's voice in the doorway, "has my spickled hin showed any signs of setting yet?"

"She's been over twa weeks," answered Dannie. "She's in that barrel there in the corner."

Mary entered the barn, removed the prop, lowered the board, and kneeling, stroked the hen, and talked softly to her. She slipped a hand under the hen, and lifted her to see the eggs. Dannie staring at Mary noted closer the fresh, cleared skin, the glossy hair, the delicately colored cheeks, and the plumpness of the bare arms. One little wisp of curl lay against the curve of her neck, just where it showed rose-pink, and looked honey sweet. And in one great surge, the repressed stream of passion in the strong man broke, and Dannie swayed against his horse. His tongue stuck to the roof of his mouth, and he caught at the harness to steady himself, while he strove to grow accustomed to the fact that Hell had opened in a new form for him. The old heart hunger for Mary Malone was back in stronger force than ever before; and because of him Jimmy lay stretched on Five Mile Hill.

"Dannie, you are just fine!" said Mary. "I've been almost wild to get home, because I thought iverything would be ruined, and instid of that it's all ixactly the way I do it. Do hurry, and get riddy for supper. Oh, it's so good to be home again! I want to make garden, and fix my flowers, and get some little chickens and turkeys into my fingers."

"I have to go home, and wash, and spruce up a bit, for ladies," said Dannie, leaving the barn.

Mary made no reply, and it came to him that she expected it. "Damned if I will!" he said, as he started home. "If she wants to come here, and force herself on me, she can, but she canna mak' me"

Just then Dannie stepped in his door, and slowly gazed about him. In a way his home was as completely transformed as hers. He washed his face and hands, and started for a better coat. His sleeping room shone with clean windows, curtained in snowy white. A freshly ironed suit of underclothing and a shirt lay on his bed. Dannie stared at them.

"She think's I'll tog up in them, and come courtin'" he growled. "I'll show her if I do! I winna touch them!"

To prove that he would not, Dannie caught them up in a wad, and threw them into a corner. That showed a clean sheet, fresh pillow, and new covers, invitingly spread back. Dannie turned as white as the pillow at which he stared.

"That's a damn plain insinuation that I'm to get into ye," he said to the bed, "and go on living here. I dinna know as that child's jabber counts. For all I know, Mary may already have picked out some town dude to bring here and farm out on me, and they'll live with the bird cage. and I can go on climbin' into ye alone."

Here was a new thought. Mary might mean only kindness to him again, as she had sent word by Jimmy she meant years ago. He might lose her for the second time. And again a wave of desire struck Dannie, and left him staggering.

"Ain't you comin', Uncle Dannie?" called the child's voice at the back door.

"What's your name, little lass?" inquired Dannie.

"Tilly," answered the little girl promptly.

"Well, Tilly, ye go tell your Aunt Mary I have been in an eelevator handlin' grain, and I'm covered wi' fine dust and chaff that sticks me. I canna come until I've had a bath, and put on clean clothing. Tell her to go ahead."

The child vanished. In a second she was back. "She said she won't do it, and take all the time you want. But I wish you'd hurry, for she won't let me either."

Dannie hurried. But the hasty bath and the fresh clothing felt so good he was in a softened mood when he approached Mary's door again. Tilly was waiting on the step, and ran to meet him. Tilly was a dream. Almost, Dannie understood why Mary had brought her. Tilly led him to the table, and pulled back a chair for him, and he lifted her into hers, and as Mary set dish after dish of food on the table, Tilly filled in every pause that threatened to grow awkward with her chatter. Dannie had been a very lonely man, and he did love Mary's cooking. Until then he had not realized how sore a trial six months of his own had been.

"If I was a praying mon, I'd ask a blessing, and thank God fra this food," said Dannie.

"What's the matter with me?" asked Mary.

"I have never yet found anything," answered Dannie. "And I do thank ye fra everything. I believe I'm most thankful of all fra the clean clothes and the clean bed. I'm afraid I was neglectin' myself, Mary."

"Will, you'll not be neglected any more," said Mary. "Things have turned over a new leaf here. For all you give, you get some return, after this. We are going to do business in a businesslike way, and divide even. I liked that bank account, pretty will, Dannie. Thank you, for that. And don't think I spint all of it. I didn't spind a hundred dollars all togither. Not the price of one horse! But it made me so happy I could fly. Home again, and the things I've always wanted, and nothing to fear. Oh, Dannie, you don't know what it manes to a woman to be always afraid! My heart is almost jumping out of my body, just with pure joy that the old fear is gone."

"I know what it means to a mon to be afraid," said Dannie. And vividly before him loomed the awful, distorted, dying face of Jimmy.

Mary guessed, and her bright face clouded.

"Some day, Dannie, we must have a little talk," she said, "and clear up a few things neither of us understand. 'Til thin we will just farm, and be partners, and be as happy as iver we can. I don't know as you mean to, but if you do, I warn you right now that you need niver mintion the name of Jimmy Malone to me again, for any reason."

Dannie left the cabin abruptly.

"Now you gone and made him mad!" reproached Tilly.

During the past winter Mary had lived with other married people for the first time, and she had imbibed some of Mrs. Dolan's philosophy.

"Whin he smells the biscuit I mane to make for breakfast, he'll get glad again," she said, and he did.

But first he went home, and tried to learn where he stood. WAS HE TRULY RESPONSIBLE FOR JIMMY'S DEATH? Yes. If he had acted like a man, he could have saved Jimmy. He was responsible. Did he want to marry Mary? Did he? Dannie reached empty arms to empty space, and groaned aloud. Would she marry him? Well, now, would she? After years of neglect and sorrow, Dannie knew that Mary had learned to prefer him to Jimmy. But almost any man would have been preferable to a woman, to Jimmy. Jimmy was distinctly a man's man. A jolly good fellow, but he would not deny himself anything, no matter what it cost his wife, and he had been very hard to live with. Dannie admitted that. So Mary had come to prefer him to Jimmy, that was sure; but it was not a question between him and Jimmy, now. It was between him, and any marriageable man that Mary might fancy.

He had grown old, and gray, and wrinkled, though he was under forty. Mary had grown round, and young, and he had never seen her looking so beautiful.

Surely she would want a man now as young, and as fresh as herself; and she might want to live in town after a while, if she grew tired of the country. Could he remember Jimmy's dreadful death, realize that he was responsible for it, and make love to his wife? No, she was sacred to Jimmy. Could he live beside her, and lose her to another man for the second time? No, she belonged to him. It was almost daybreak when Dannie remembered the fresh bed, and lay down for a few hours' rest.

But there was no rest for Dannie, and after tossing about until dawn he began his work. When he carried the milk into the cabin, and smelled the biscuit, he fulfilled Mary's prophecy, got glad again, and came to breakfast. Then he went about his work. But as the day wore on, he repeatedly heard the voice of the woman and the child, combining in a chorus of laughter. From the little front porch, the green bird warbled and trilled. Neighbors who had heard of her return came up the lane to welcome a happy Mary Malone. The dead dreariness of winter melted before the spring sun, and in Dannie's veins the warm blood swept up, as the sap flooded the trees, and in spite of himself he grew gladder and yet gladder.

He now knew how he had missed Mary. How he had loathed that empty, silent cabin. How remorse and heart hunger had gnawed at his vitals, and he decided that he would go on just as Mary had said, and let things drift; and when she was ready to have the talk with him she had mentioned, he would hear what she had to say. And as he thought over these things, he caught himself watching for furrows that Jimmy was not making on the other side of the field. He tried to talk to the robins and blackbirds instead of Jimmy, but they were not such good company. And when the day was over, he tried not to be glad that he was going to the shining eyes of Mary Malone, a good supper, and a clean bed, and it was not in the heart of man to do it.

The summer wore on, autumn came, and the year Tilly had spoken of was over. Dannie went his way, doing the work of two men, thinking of everything, planning for everything, and he was all the heart of Mary Malone could desire, save her lover. By little Mary pieced it out. Dannie never mentioned fishing; he had lost his love for the river. She knew that he frequently took walks to Five Mile Hill. His devotion to Jimmy's memory was unswerving. And at last it came to her, that in death as in life, Jimmy Malone was separating them. She began to realize that there might be things she did not know. What had Jimmy told the priest? Why had Father Michael refused to confess Jimmy until he sent Dannie to him? What had passed between them? If it was what she had thought all year, why did it not free Dannie to her? If there was something more, what was it?

Surely Dannie loved her. Much as he had cared for Jimmy, he had vowed that everything was for her first. She was eager to be his wife, and something bound him. One day, she decided to ask him. The next, she shrank in burning confusion, for when Jimmy Malone had asked for her love, she had admitted to him that she loved Dannie, and Jimmy had told her that it was no use, Dannie did not care for girls, and that he had said he wished she would not thrust herself upon him. On the strength of that statement Mary married Jimmy inside five weeks, and spent years in bitter repentance.

That was the thing which held her now. If Dannie knew what she did, and did not care to marry her, how could she mention it? Mary began to grow pale, and lose sleep, and Dannie said the heat of the summer had tired her, and suggested that she go to Mrs. Dolan's for a weeks rest. The fact that he was willing, and possibly anxious to send her away for a whole week, angered Mary. She went.

Chapter XI

THE POT OF GOLD

M ARY had not been in the Dolan home an hour until Katy knew all she could tell of her trouble. Mrs. Dolan was practical. "Go to see Father Michael," she said. "What's he for but to hilp us. Go ask him what Jimmy told him. Till him how you feel and what you know. He can till you what Dannie knows and thin you will understand where you are at."

Mary was on the way before Mrs. Dolan fully finished. She went to the priest's residence and asked his housekeeper to inquire if he would see her. He would, and Mary entered his presence strangely calm and self-possessed. This was the last fight she knew of that she could make for happiness, and if she lost, happiness was over for her. She had need of all her wit and she knew it. Father Michael began laughing as he shook hands.

"Now look here, Mary," he said, "I've been expecting you. I warn you before you begin that I cannot sanction your marriage to a Protestant."

"Oh, but I'm going to convart him!" cried Mary so quickly that the priest laughed harder than ever.

"So that's the lay of the land!" he chuckled. "Well, if you'll guarantee that, I'll give in. When shall I read the banns?"

"Not until we get Dannie's consint," answered Mary, and for the first her voice wavered.

Father Michael looked his surprise. "Tut! Tut!" he said. "And is Dannie dilatory?"

"Dannie is the finest man that will ever live in this world," said Mary, "but he don't want to marry me."

"To my certain knowledge Dannie has loved you all your life," said Father Michael. "He wants nothing here or hereafter as he wants to marry you."

"Thin why don't he till me so?" sobbed Mary, burying her burning face in her hands.

"Has he said nothing to you?" gravely inquired the priest.

"No, he hasn't and I don't belave he intinds to," answered Mary, wiping her eyes and trying to be composed. "There is something about Jimmy that is holding him back. Mrs. Dolan thought you'd help me."

"What do you want me to do, Mary?" asked Father Michael.

"Two things," answered Mary promptly. "I want you to tell me what Jimmy confessed to you before he died, and then I want you to talk to Dannie and show him that he is free from any promise that Jimmy might have got out of him. Will you?"

"A dying confession—" began the priest.

"Yes, but I know—" broke in Mary. "I saw them fight, and I heard Jimmy till Dannie that he'd lied to him to separate us, but he turned right around and took it back and I knew Dannie belaved him thin; but he can't after Jimmy confessed it again to both of you."

"What do you mean by 'saw them fight?'" Father Michael was leaning toward Mary anxiously.

Mary told him.

"Then that is the explanation to the whole thing," said the priest. "Dannie did believe Jimmy when he took it back, and he died before he could repeat to Dannie what he had told me. And I have had the feeling that Dannie thought himself in a way to blame for Jimmy's death."

"He was not! Oh, he was not!" cried Mary Malone. "Didn't I live there with them all those years? Dannie always was good as gold to Jimmy. It was shameful the way Jimmy imposed on him, and spint his money, and took me from him. It was shameful! Shameful!"

"Be calm! Be calm!" cautioned Father Michael. "I agree with you. I am only trying to arrive at Dannie's point of view. He well might feel that he was responsible, if after humoring Jimmy like a child all his life, he at last lost his temper and dealt with him as if he were a man. If that is the case, he is of honor so fine, that he would hesitate to speak to you, no matter what he suffered. And then it is clear to me that he does not understand how Jimmy separated you in the first place."

"And lied me into marrying him, whin I told him over and over how I loved Dannie. Jimmy Malone took iverything I had to give, and he left me alone for fiftane years, with my three little dead babies, that died because I'd no heart to desire life for thim, and he took my youth, and he took my womanhood, and he took my man—" Mary arose in primitive rage. "You naden't bother!" she said. "I'm going straight to Dannie meself."

"Don't!" said Father Michael softly. "Don't do that, Mary! It isn't the accepted way. There is a better! Let him come to you."

"But he won't come! He don't know! He's in Jimmy's grip tighter in death than he was in life." Mary began to sob again.

"He will come," said Father Michael. "Be calm! Wait a little, my child. After all these years, don't spoil a love that has been almost unequaled in holiness and beauty, by anger at the dead. Let me go to Dannie. We are good friends. I can tell him Jimmy made a confession to me, that he was trying to repeat to him, when punishment, far more awful than anything you have suffered, overtook him. Always remember, Mary, he died unshriven!" Mary began to shiver. "Your suffering is over," continued the priest. "You have many good years yet that you may spend with Dannie; God will give you living children, I am sure. Think of the years Jimmy's secret has hounded and driven him! Think of the penalty he must pay before he gets a glimpse of paradise, if he be not eternally lost!"

"I have!" exclaimed Mary. "And it is nothing to the fact that he took Dannie from me, and yet kept him in my home while he possessed me himsilf for years. May he burn——"

"Mary! Let that suffice!" cried the priest. "He will! The question now is, shall I go to Dannie?"

"Will you till him just what Jimmy told you? Will you till him that I have loved him always?"

"Yes," said Father Michael.

"Will you go now?"

"I cannot! I have work. I will come early in the morning."

"You will till him ivirything?" she repeated.

"I will," promised Father Michael.

Mary went back to Mrs. Dolan's comforted. She was anxious to return home at once, but at last consented to spend the day. Now that she was sure Dannie did not know the truth, her heart warmed toward him. She was anxious to comfort and help him in the long struggle which she saw that he must have endured. By late afternoon she could bear it no longer and started back to Rainbow Bottom in time to prepare supper.

For the first hour after Mary had gone Dannie whistled to keep up his courage. By the second he had no courage to keep. By the third he was indulging in the worst fit of despondency he ever had known. He had told her to stay a week. A week! It would be an eternity! There alone again! Could he bear it? He got through to mid- afternoon some way, and then in jealous fear and foreboding he became almost frantic. One way or the other, this thing must be settled. Fiercer raged the storm within him and at last toward evening it became unendurable.

At its height the curling smoke from the chimney told him that Mary had come home. An unreasoning joy seized him. He went to the barn and listened. He could hear her moving about preparing supper. As he watched she came to the well for water and before she returned to the cabin she stood looking over the fields as if trying to locate him. Dannie's blood ran hotly and his pulses were leaping. "Go to her! Go to her now!" demanded passion, struggling to break leash. "You killed Jimmy! You murdered your friend!" cried conscience, with unyielding insistence. Poor Dannie gave one last glance at Mary, and then turned, and for the second time he ran from her as if pursued by demons. But this time he went straight to Five Mile Hill, and the grave of Jimmy Malone.

He sat down on it, and within a few feet of Jimmy's bones, Dannie took his tired head in his hands, and tried to think, and for the life of him, he could think but two things. That he had killed Jimmy, and that to live longer without Mary would kill him. Hour after hour he fought with his lifelong love for Jimmy and his lifelong love for Mary. Night came on, the frost bit, the wind chilled, and the little brown owls screeched among the gravestones, and Dannie battled on. Morning came, the sun arose, and shone on Dannie, sitting numb with drawn face and bleeding heart.

Mary prepared a fine supper the night before, and patiently waited, and when Dannie did not come, she concluded that he had gone to town, without knowing that she had returned. Tilly grew sleepy, so she put the child to bed, and presently she went herself. Father Michael would make everything right in the morning. But in the morning Dannie was not there, and had not been. Mary became alarmed. She was very nervous by the time Father Michael arrived. He decided to go to the nearest neighbor, and ask when Dannie had been seen last. As he turned from the lane into the road a man of that neighborhood was passing on his wagon, and the priest hailed him, and asked if he knew where Dannie Macnoun was.

"Back in Five Mile Hill, a man with his head on his knees, is a- settin' on the grave of Jimmy Malone, and I allow that would be Dannie Macnoun, the damn fool!" he said.

Father Michael went back to the cabin, and told Mary he had learned where Dannie was, and to have no uneasiness, and he would go to see him immediately.

"And first of all you'll tell him how Jimmy lied to him?"

"I will!" said the priest.

He entered the cemetery, and walked slowly to the grave of Jimmy Malone. Dannie lifted his head, and stared at him.

"I saw you," said Father Michael, "and I came in to speak with you." He took Dannie's hand. "You are here at this hour to my surprise."

"I dinna know that ye should be surprised at my comin' to sit by Jimmy at ony time," coldly replied Dannie. "He was my only friend in life, and another mon so fine I'll never know. I often come here."

The priest shifted his weight from one foot to the other, and then he sat down on a grave near Dannie. "For a year I have been waiting to talk with you," he said.

Dannie wiped his face, and lifting his hat, ran his fingers through his hair, as if to arouse himself. His eyes were dull and listless. "I am afraid I am no fit to talk sensibly," he said. "I am much troubled. Some other time——"

"Could you tell me your trouble?" asked Father Michael.

Dannie shook his head.

"I have known Mary Malone all her life," said the priest softly, "and been her confessor. I have known Jimmy Malone all his life, and heard his dying confession. I know what it was he was trying to tell you when he died. Think again!"

Dannie Macnoun stood up. He looked at the priest intently. "Did ye come here purposely to find me?"

"Yes."

"What do ye want?"

"To clear your mind of all trouble, and fill your heart with love, and great peace, and rest. Our Heavenly Father knows that you need peace of heart, and rest, Dannie."

"To fill my heart wi' peace, ye will have to prove to me that I'm no responsible fra the death of Jimmy Malone; and to give it rest, ye will have to prove to me that I'm free to marry his wife. Ye can do neither of those things."

"I can do both," said the priest calmly. "My son, that is what I came to do."

Dannie's face grew whiter and whiter, as the blood receded, and his big hands gripped at his sides.

"Aye, but ye canna!" he cried desperately. "Ye canna!"

"I can," said the priest. "Listen to me! Did Jimmy get anything at all said to you?"

"He said, `Mary,' then he choked on the next word, then he gasped out `yours,' and it was over."

"Have you any idea what he was trying to tell you?"

"Na!" answered Dannie. "He was mortal sick, and half delirious, and I paid little heed. If he lived, he would tell me when he was better. If he died, nothing mattered, fra I was responsible, and better friend mon never had. There was nothing on earth Jimmy would na have done for me. He was so big hearted, so generous! My God, how I have missed him! How I have missed him!"

"Your faith in Jimmy is strong," ventured the bewildered priest, for he did not see his way.

Dannie lifted his head. The sunshine was warming him, and his thoughts were beginning to clear.

"My faith in Jimmy Malone is so strong," he said, "that if I lost it, I never should trust another living mon. He had his faults to others, I admit that, but he never had ony to me. He was my friend, and above my life I loved him. I wad gladly have died to save him."

"And yet you say you are responsible for his death!"

"Let me tell ye!" cried Dannie eagerly, and began on the story the priest wanted to hear from him. As he finished Father Michael's face lighted.

"What folly!" he said, "that a man of your intelligence should torture yourself with the thought of responsibility in a case like that. Any one would have claimed the fish in those circumstances. Priest that I am, I would have had it, even if I fought for it. Any man would! And as for what followed, it was bound to come! He was a tortured man, and a broken one. If he had not lain out that night, he would a few nights later. It was not in your power to save him. No man can be saved from himself, Dannie. Did what he said make no impression on you?"

"Enough that I would have killed him with my naked hands if he had na taken it back. Of course he had to retract! If I believed that of Jimmy, after the life we lived together, I would curse God and mon, and break fra the woods, and live and dee there alone."

"Then what was he trying to tell you when he died?" asked the bewildered priest.

"To take care of Mary, I judge."

"Not to marry her; and take her for your own?"

Dannie began to tremble.

"Remember, I talked with him first," said Father Michael, "and what he confessed to me, he knew was final. He died before he could talk to you, but I think it is time to tell you what he wanted to say. He—he—was trying—trying to tell you, that there was nothing but love in his heart for you. That he did not in any way blame you. That—that Mary was yours. That you were free to take her. That——"

"What!" cried Dannie wildly. "Are ye sure? Oh, my God!"

"Perfectly sure!" answered Father Michael. "Jimmy knew how long and faithfully you had loved Mary, and she had loved you——"

"Mary had loved me? Carefu', mon! Are ye sure?"

"I know," said Father Michael convincingly. "I give you my priestly word, I know, and Jimmy knew, and was altogether willing. He loved you deeply, as he could love any one, Dannie, and he blamed you for nothing at all. The only thing that would have brought Jimmy any comfort in dying, was to know that you would end your life with Mary, and not hate his memory."

"Hate!" cried Dannie. "Hate! Father Michael, if ye have come to tell me that Jimmy na held me responsible fra his death, and was willing fra me to have Mary, your face looks like the face of God to me!" Dannie gripped the priest's hand. "Are ye sure? Are ye sure, mon?" He almost lifted Father Michael from the ground.

"I tell you, I know! Go and be happy!"

"Some ither day I will try to thank ye," said Dannie, turning away. "Noo, I'm in a little of a hurry." He was half way to the gate when he turned back. "Does Mary know this?" he asked.

"She does," said the priest. "You are one good man, Dannie, go and be happy, and may the blessing of God go with you."

Dannie lifted his hat.

"And Jimmy, too," he said, "put Jimmy in, Father Michael."

"May the peace of God rest the troubled soul of Jimmy Malone," said Father Michael, and not being a Catholic, Dannie did not know that from the blessing for which he asked.

He hurried away with the brightness of dawn on his lined face, which looked almost boyish under his whitening hair.

Mary Malone was at the window, and turmoil and bitterness were beginning to burn in her heart again. Maybe the priest had not found Dannie. Maybe he was not coming. Maybe a thousand things. Then he WAS coming. Coming straight and sure. Coming across the fields, and leaping fences at a bound. Coming with such speed and force as comes the strong man, fifteen years denied. Mary's heart began to jar, and thump, and waves of happiness surged over her. And then she saw that look of dawn, of serene delight on the face of the man, and she stood aghast. Dannie threw wide the door, and crossed her threshold with outstretched arms.

"Is it true?" he panted. "That thing Father Michael told me, is it true? Will ye be mine, Mary Malone? At last will you be mine? Oh, my girl, is the beautiful thing that the priest told me true?"

"THE BEAUTIFUL THING THAT THE PRIEST TOLD HIM!"

Mary Malone swung a chair before her, and stepped back. "Wait!" she cried sharply. "There must be some mistake. Till me ixactly what Father Michael told you?"

"He told me that Jimmy na held me responsible fra his death. That he loved me when he died. That he was willing I should have ye! Oh, Mary, wasna that splendid of him. Wasna he a grand mon? Mary, come to me. Say that it's true! Tell me, if ye love me."

Mary Malone stared wide-eyed at Dannie, and gasped for breath.

Dannie came closer. At last he had found his tongue. "Fra the love of mercy, if ye are comin' to me, come noo, Mary" he begged. "My arms will split if they dinna get round ye soon, dear. Jimmy told ye fra me, sixteen years ago, how I loved ye, and he told me when he came back how sorry ye were fra me, and he—he almost cried when he told me. I never saw a mon feel so. Grand old Jimmy! No other mon like him!"

Mary drew back in desperation.

"You see here, Dannie Micnoun!" she screamed. "You see here——"

"I do," broke in Dannie. "I'm lookin'! All I ever saw, or see now, or shall see till I dee is 'here,' when 'here' is ye, Mary Malone. Oh! If a woman ever could understand what passion means to a mon! If ye knew what I have suffered through all these years, you'd end it, Mary Malone."

Mary gave the chair a shove. "Come here, Dannie," she said. Dannie cleared the space between them. Mary set her hands against his breast. "One minute," she panted. "Just one! I have loved you all me life, me man. I niver loved any one but you. I niver wanted any one but you. I niver hoped for any Hivin better than I knew I'd find in your arms. There was a mistake. There was an awful mistake, when I married Jimmy. I'm not tillin' you now, and I niver will, but you must realize that! Do you understand me?"

"Hardly," breathed Dannie. "Hardly!"

"Will, you can take your time if you want to think it out, because that's all I'll iver till you. There was a horrible mistake. It was YOU I loved, and wanted to marry. Now bend down to me, Dannie Micnoun, because I'm going to take your head on me breast and kiss your dear face until I'm tired," said Mary Malone.

An hour later Father Michael came leisurely down the lane, and the peace of God was with him.

A radiant Mary went out to meet him.

"You didn't till him!" she cried accusingly. "You didn't till him!"

The priest laid a hand on her head.

"Mary, the greatest thing in the whole world is self-sacrifice," he said. "The pot at the foot of the rainbow is just now running over with the pure gold of perfect contentment. But had you and I done such a dreadful thing as to destroy the confidence of a good man in his friend, your heart never could know such joy as it now knows in this sacrifice of yours; and no such blessed, shining light could illumine your face. That is what I wanted to see. I said to myself as I came along, 'She will try, but she will learn, as I did, that she cannot look in his eyes and undeceive him. And when she becomes reconciled, her face will be so good to see.' And it is. You did not tell him either, Mary Malone!"

Echo Library
www.echo-library.com

Echo Library uses advanced digital print-on-demand technology to build and preserve an exciting world class collection of rare and out-of-print books, making them readily available for everyone to enjoy.

Situated just yards from Teddington Lock on the River Thames, Echo Library was founded in 2005 by Tom Cherrington, a specialist dealer in rare and antiquarian books with a passion for literature.

Please visit our website for a complete catalogue of our books, which includes foreign language titles.

The Right to Read

Echo Library actively supports the Royal National Institute for the Blind's Right to Read initiative by publishing a comprehensive range of Large Print (16 point Tiresias font as recommended by the RNIB) and Clear Print (13 point Tiresias font) titles for those who find standard print difficult to read.

Customer Service

If there is a serious error in the text or layout please send details to feedback@echo-library.com and we will supply a corrected copy. If there is a printing fault or the book is damaged please refer to your supplier.